Fatal Conception

DANIELLE LYDIC

Fatal Conception
© 2022 Danielle Lydic

This is a work of fiction. Names, characters, organizations, places, events, and incidents are products of the author's imagination and used fictitiously. Any resemblance to actual people or events is purely coincidental.

No part of this book may be reproduced, stored in a retrieval system or transmitted in any form or by any means, electronic, mechanical, photocopying, recording , or otherwise, without the written permission of the author.

Scripture taken from The Holy Bible, New King James Version®. Copyright © 1982 by Thomas Nelson. Used by permission. All rights reserved.

Lifehopeandtruth.com – Used by permission of Life, Hope & Truth

ISBN 978-1-66787-230-8

eBook ISBN 978-1-66787-231-5

Jeremiah 1:5

"Before I formed you in the womb I knew you;

Before you were born I sanctified you."

Darcy

I felt it before I saw the blood. It was a warm sensation running down my thigh and I didn't have to look to know what was happening. This was my punishment, and I wanted it to run out of me and take my life with it…

Four months earlier, I never would have imagined the dark, lonely place I would soon find refuge in would be from my own doing. It all started innocently enough… doesn't everything though? I thought I had it all figured out. I was in my senior year of high school. I was feeling great and getting ready to map out my future. I still remember the night that changed everything. It is vividly imprinted in my mind; the memory so real that it could have happened yesterday. It was the middle of September and I was excited for the first night of the local fair. Living in a rural area meant when the fair came everyone would be there. I spent the afternoon, with my little sister, Midge, curling each other's hair and trying to figure out what to wear. When we got to the fairgrounds, I remember the breeze blowing our hair back, the warm, humid air making my flannel stifling. I unbuttoned the top buttons of my flannel; something I normally felt self-conscious about because of my large bust size. Maybe it was from wearing my work uniform all summer and being stuck inside, but a part of me wanted to get some attention.

Midge grabbed my hand and led me into the crowd. We were trying to figure out what we wanted to do first. Should we get something to eat or look for our friends? We were so tempted to grab a funnel cake; the smells from Mister D's Funnel Cake Stand nearly made the decision for us. I could almost taste the fried dough and powdered sugar. Midge won the debate though when she declared we could share one later. We ended up getting in line for some blooming onions when we saw a group of our friends from school.

Someone from school who knew Midge ran over and grabbed her shouting she had to join them to check out the log sawing contest because, "The guys with chainsaws were so hot!" Ugh, I was not interested in that so I rolled my eyes and called my friend Tina asking her to wait in line with me. While we were in line, she was telling me that Drake Rodman, who went to school in a nearby town, was there tonight and she was so excited. The rumor mill indicated he was single now. His girlfriend hadn't been to any of the football games recently, and he even came to the fair alone. This was big news. Drake was the star player of the football team; even our school's cheerleaders threw themselves at him. It was disgusting, I thought. They all acted so shallow and gossiped behind all the player's backs. As soon as any of the football players were around the cheerleaders would throw themselves at them. Whoever received the most attention from the football players would be the winner of some kind of simple-minded beauty contest. That kind of stuff just didn't matter to me, I had my friends and family. Tonight, I had the fair, and it was fantastic.

Tina and I rejoined some of the others from our school by the barns and joked around. I was trying to dare someone to get tattoo advice from a carnie when we heard a loud whooping from the direction of the rides. It was a couple guys from the football team. They were being loud and asking where the best place to go and get drunk was. I didn't notice him walk up to me, but I could feel his gaze. When I looked to my left, I saw Drake standing there. He was staring at me. To be honest, it felt intimidating. I wasn't used to that kind of attention. I tended to be quiet and preferred to be the listener of the group, the 'good girl'. Everyone liked to try and get me to smoke or get high and would get a howl out of it when I acted shy.

He jokingly put his arm around my shoulder and said, "Why haven't I seen you cheering at your school? I know you're a cheerleader with a body like that." I immediately blushed and everyone laughed.

"No, I'm not a cheerleader. I figured my test scores were too high for them to want me. My name is Darcy." Drake kept his arm around my shoulder and just shrugged.

"Well Darcy, I think you are just the cutest."

His arm felt like a hundred pounds. I was so uncomfortable. At the same time, it felt good to have some attention. My younger sister is the one with the loud, infectious personality that everyone is drawn to. She always gets the attention from everyone we hang out with. It was nice to have someone actually notice me. Some of the guys passed water bottles around. Tina asked me to try some. I put the bottle up to my nose and immediately could smell the Vodka. For some unknown reason, I took a long drink. I felt like Drake saw something in me he liked, and for some crazy reason I wanted to make sure I was embodying the "cheerleader persona" he was into.

About an hour later, some of our friends were ready to take the fun to a nearby abandoned barn; the plan was to make a fire and keep the party going. At this time of night, I would usually start connecting with my sister or meeting up with my parents to head home; but, I was feeling loose and energized. I texted my sister and asked if she could ride home with mom and dad, and asked her to let them know I was going home with Tina. We all piled into some vehicles. When I went to get into one of the cars, Drake pulled me into a different one and had me sit on his lap. I'd never been this close to a guy before. It was intoxicating. Looking back on things now, I know it was because of the alcohol. I remember feeling so wired and aware of every touch, our bodies bumping into each other as the car navigated the unkempt dirt road. While we drove, he kept his hands low on my sides and I held onto the seat in front of me. I could feel him getting hard under me. I felt so powerful knowing that I could elicit that kind of reaction. Drake Rodman was interested in me! It was so alluring. The only experience I'd ever had with a guy was last year when Sam Doughterman and I made an awkward attempt at kissing after the homecoming dance. It was so off-putting that I decided it would be better to wait until college, when I could go on proper dates with guys who didn't sweat bullets just because your cleavage was showing.

When we got to the barn, some of the others started finding old wood to start a fire. Chuck Dietman brought out some of those cheap wine boxes. Everyone thought it was hilarious to tilt their heads back so he could come around and fill their mouths instead of using cups. By this time, I was feeling a little dizzy so I stepped back from the fire and leaned against an old fence post. Drake was still sitting by the fire but I could feel his gaze on me the entire time. When I looked up, he was staring straight at me. His stare was intense and I shifted on my feet uncertain of how to stand. Instead, I turned and walked around the corner of the barn looking for a good place where I could squat to pee.

I wandered a couple yards into the cornfield that grew behind the old barn. I had just finished and stood up to button my jeans when Drake was suddenly standing in front of me. He looked down to see my pants unbuttoned and slowly smiled, "I knew you wanted me to follow you back here." I wasn't sure what to say, I was aware that from the sound of music we were actually farther from the group than I intended to be.

Trying to be cute I said, "Well, you would be the expert in reading a play, I guess." I cleared my throat into my hand and wasn't quite sure what to do next. I was feeling uncomfortable and didn't like the way he was looking at me. What had been funny exchanges and little glances earlier was now over. I felt his overall demeanor changing and I pretended to love the song I heard playing. I was trying to dance back to the fire when he reached out and pulled me back into the cornfield.

The next thing I knew, his hands were all over me and he was pulling me closer to him. With one hand, he was holding me against his body and the other was pushing into my pants, into my underwear. I remember letting out a gasp at the total shock of it, as his rough fingers pushed into me. He must have mistaken the sound for pleasure or some kind of assurance because the next thing he did was take my shoulders and push me down to my knees. It was like slow motion. He held my shoulder down with one hand and with the other hand pulled himself out of his pants and pushed into my mouth. Tears were coming down my face as he pushed harder. When he pulled out, I had to lean over to cough. The next thing I knew, he shoved me back and was yanking my pants down. I was trying to cough and say no but I couldn't say anything, it was like my mouth and brain weren't communicating. My heart was beating wildly and before I could even react he was trying to push inside of me. I didn't think it would work and he was going to give up. He spit into his hand and then rubbed it all over me, I turned my head away feeling dirty. He started pushing again and I could feel him going inside of me. The pain raced up my body and I dug my fingers into the dirt. He was on top of me and his face was twisted, his eyes were closed and his fingers were squeezing into my shoulders. I tried breathing through my mouth so I wouldn't have to smell his hot beer breath as he blew it out on my face. The tears were coming now and I focused on the ground and where the corn stalks towered over me. I could smell the smoke from the fire and could barely make out the sounds of my friends laughing and singing out loud. I tried to focus on anything except what was happening. After what seemed like forever, he reached down to my hips and pushed even further into me and then it was over. His face was covered in sweat and it rubbed against me as he put his head down and then set up and started pulling his pants up. I was still laying there. Staring to the side, into nothingness. When I didn't say anything, he got up and walked away.

    Once it was quiet, I sat up slowly. I saw that my tears had made a little wet patch in the dirt. Then I quickly realized that was also where I relieved myself earlier. As I sat up and began putting my pants on, I took inventory of the pain in my body. I felt aches all over, especially between my legs. There was a small amount of blood on my thigh and there was more on the ground below me. When I went to take my next breath, I immediately vomited all over and fell to my knees crying, while I continued throwing up. I tried to get all the vileness he left inside of me out, as I pushed my fingers down my throat. I heard my friend Tina call out to me and I just turned and started running deeper into the cornfield. I was too embarrassed to be seen and there was no way I was going back like this for them all to see how disgusting I really was. I ran until I broke through the other side of the field. Then I sent Tina a text telling her I just ended up feeling sick and had my older brother pick me up. I found a place to lay down and cried myself to sleep.

    The next morning, I texted my sister and had her pick me up. I knew she would be excited to come and get me. Since she got her license, she has been volunteering for every little errand my parents needed done. Her smile quickly disappeared when she saw me. That was when I realized what a mess I must have looked like. My clothes were dirty, I smelled like smoke, urine and vomit. My hair was matted and my face was swollen from crying. My mouth was dry. I was probably dehydrated or very close to becoming dehydrated. I just told her I got carried away and got too drunk the night before. That I had spent the night throwing up and was too embarrassed to let anyone know. I made her promise not to tell anyone and to help me sneak back into the house without being seen. She looked concerned, but nodded a 'yes', in agreement. As I showered later, I let the hot water scald my skin. I still felt cold and dirty. When the water started to run cold, I got out and put on a robe. I crawled into bed and pretended I never left the day before. Hoping that when I woke up, everything would be like it was before the fair.

As it turns out, the next week at school was just like any other week. With one exception, everyone was talking about how Drake would miss the rest of the football season. Something our football team was happy about, because now they wouldn't have such stiff competition. They were saying that when Drake came back from the cornfield, he stumbled and fell over a log. He put his hands out to stop himself as he fell. He hit the ground hard, breaking his wrist in the process. He started screaming. Constantly reminding everyone this was his throwing arm. Someone ended up taking him to the hospital. Everyone gave him so much attention that they completely forgot I was back there at the same time as him. In a way, they forgot I was even there at all. It became known as the night that Drake got drunk, messed up his wrist and lost his spot on the football team.

I went back to being my quiet self, and became more focused than ever on my grades and college prep. After school, I usually avoided everyone and went straight home. I blocked it all out and was beginning to convince myself that night never happened. For the next month, all my spare time was devoted to studying and reading.

It was working too, until the morning of Mr. Gomez's first period class when he came in with a steaming cup of coffee and an egg and sausage croissant. As he approached my seat, the smell of his breakfast drifted towards me. I threw up all over his brown loafers. The school nurse had me lay down on the cot in the back of her room, while she called my mother, to tell her about my upset stomach, and made arrangements for me to go home.

Then it dawned on me. When was my last period? It was Labor Day weekend. I remember being annoyed that I had to help out at the Church picnic by setting up the tables. All I really wanted to do was go somewhere and sleep for the day. I knew there was no doubt. I was pregnant. My cycle was always on time and here I was at least a week late. At this realization, I felt nauseous all over again and I thought I was going to pass out. The room was spinning so fast. How could this happen? This thing was growing in me? I felt humiliated all over again. Just when I thought I could get through that night. Not only did I make bad choices that night. I let myself get into an awful predicament with Drake. I know I was careless in taking care of myself afterwards and was just as stupid for not thinking about the fact that I could get pregnant. Like someone not washing their hands well when the person they are with is sick, I had caught something from Drake. Like a virus, he spread it to me, and I had caught it; because of my own stupidity. Now I had to deal with it. There was no way I was going to be able to tell my parents about this, and Drake probably won't even remember me. No one would believe me. I had to deal with this on my own, and be rid of it once and for all.

My mom picked me up from school and when we got home, she did her usual tea and toast by the bedside and *"call me if you need me"* reassurance. I waited until she left to figure out the next part of my plan. I knew there was no one I could talk to about this. My family was very strict about drinking and dating. I knew they would be disappointed in my choices that night. They would also believe that I got what I deserved because of my actions. I know they would be so embarrassed in front of everybody at church. Ugh. I couldn't even imagine having this huge baby belly and having to go to school or be around other people when they would be judging me or talking about me behind my back. Besides, we don't talk about feelings in this family and it wouldn't be too much of a stretch to think I could become an outsider in my own home. I've often wondered this about some of the homeless people I've seen on the streets. Was it easier to have the judgements and harsh words yelled at them from strangers than the words from their own family? Was it easier to live on the street facing scrutiny from nobody of significance?

I remember the time I got my first period and I had to go to my mom and ask her for some tampons. She got so weird and just bought me these extra large pads and told me tampons were not for proper women. She talked in hushed whispers like it was a dirty secret. After she gave me some pads and left me alone, I remember feeling so embarrassed in my own body that from then on whenever I had my period, I made sure not to talk about it. I would close myself off from everyone. I even felt like my mom must have told my dad because he never seemed to get close to me anymore. Almost like my change into womanhood made me a leper that he couldn't come close to. Yeah, I was definitely on my own with this even though it was ironic because there isn't any more blood that would scare my family away from me.

While I had the alone time for the next couple days with this "stomach bug", I began using my time to research how I could solve this problem. I researched how to prevent a miscarriage, and then I did the OPPOSITE! I read that smoking cigarettes and consuming energy drinks were bad, while pregnant. When everyone was gone for the day, I took the car to the Sip N Get two towns over and bought two packs of cigarettes and some energy drinks. Then, I proceeded to chain smoke in the woods behind the house and then chug energy drinks. I smoked and drank for two days straight and then I really felt like crap.

I knew that wouldn't work long term, so I decided to do the next worst thing, to starve whatever was growing in me. I stopped eating. On top of that, I started exercising every chance I got. My sister was usually the athletic one, while I was considered the smart one, but when she would get up in the morning to run I laced up with her. Even with all the stress I was putting my body through, nothing happened, and I still didn't get my period. I was beyond frustrated and getting scared. By now, almost three months had passed since my last period. Even though I was starving myself and exercising all the time, I felt like my pants were not getting any looser. Then, one Friday, I was standing in my bedroom when it happened – I couldn't button the top of my jeans. I froze and stared at myself in the mirror.

This was not going away. To make matters worse, I felt like crap every day. I was like a zombie wandering through the day in search of my next meal. I refused to let myself eat, with the exception of crackers or water. I could barely focus because I was so tired and felt nauseous all the time. Nobody even seemed to notice that I was suffering. During dinner, I would move the food around on my plate and hope my parents would notice. My dad kept his eyes on the newspaper and my mother would chat away about her day. Did they just assume I was going through some weird teenage phase? Like that time my older brother would barely utter a syllable the whole day and then go to his room and play sad country songs until my father told him to go to bed. Maybe, if I brought them a failing report card, my parents would look at me and be mad because I wasn't fitting into their smart daughter mold anymore. Isn't that what's important, good grades and working hard? Who cares if your daughter is having a breakdown right in front of you.

That's when I knew what I had to do. After I stepped out of the shower that night, I caught sight of my reflection in the mirror. I locked eyes with myself. I could hear a voice in the back of my mind, encouraging me that I was strong enough to do what needed to be done. The girl in the mirror would take care of this problem so I could get back to my life and my future. She would take on my problems so I wouldn't have to. So I could blend back into the background of my life and my parents' plan for me.

I waited until everyone was asleep in the house. Then I quietly opened my laptop, with shaky hands and creeping anxiety, I typed in the words Abortion Clinics Near Me… The first choice was almost a relief because it was two hours away. It was far away in a big city with little chance of running into any one I knew. Even though I was looking at this website in my room, in the dark, in the dead of night, I still felt like someone was going to shout, "I see you! I know what you are doing!" Was it Him? I tried to shove down the guilt I was feeling and remember that I had to do this because this was the only way I could really honor my parents. Wasn't that a commandment? Shouldn't I be making them happy?

As I searched for abortion clinics, my mind wanders back to a time my church protested on their front lawn. My mother made my sister and I stand there and hold up signs that read "A Heartbeat is Life" and "Abortion stops a Beating Heart". I remember we waved the signs at cars and then everybody went inside for doughnuts and coffee and smiled at each other like their good deed for the day was done. Did they really even care? Wouldn't I be judged for being pregnant anyway? What would it matter if I wasn't? At least, if I wasn't pregnant anymore, nobody would know except God. Didn't he forgive anyway? That's what I told myself as I typed in the address into my phone so I could drive out there the next chance I got.

The following week I mustered up the courage to get this over with. I took my shoebox, which served as my bank, down from my top shelf, in the closet, and counted out close to $200. This should be enough, right? I mean, it was not something that took a long time, I only needed to take a pill and see a doctor real quick. So I figured it would be enough. Instead of turning left out of my driveway and heading to the high school, I turned right and drove towards the city. Memories of past trips to the zoo and concerts were now being overshadowed by my guilt.

The medical complex was easy to find. Pulling up to the gray industrial building, I had the vague sense it was like me. Wanting to be concealed, to blend in, to not let others see it for what it really was, trying to mask the evil inside – what was lurking within. I had to call on the strength of the girl in the mirror, and have her take over for me. She would have the courage to do this for me.

I let her walk me to the front desk and ask in a strong voice, "Can I be seen by a doctor?"

The receptionist looked up impatiently, "Do you have an appointment?"

Shoot, I thought, I didn't even think to make an appointment. But I replied in a pleading voice, "I'm sorry, I don't, but I really need help and I just drove 2 hours to get here. Is there anyone I can see?"

She took a deep breath and asked me to sit down. She said she would be right back. I sat on the edge of the plastic seat. I had to keep wiping my palms on the front of my hoodie because I was afraid I would leave wet marks on the seat. My hands were sweating that bad.

At last, the door opened and a small framed woman, with her brown hair pinned up in an orderly bun, asked me to come with her. She took me to a room in the back, which I assumed was her office. I sat in front of her desk looking at her certificates lining the wall. She introduced herself as Dr. Woodren, and asked how she could help me. I explained that it had been over 3 months since my last period. I was a senior in High School and there was no way I could go on like this. I needed help. Despite my best efforts, I started to cry right there in front of her. I reached into my pocket and pulled out my money and said, " I can pay for everything, please just help me." She didn't move for the money; but rather, leaned back in her chair instead – considering me. Then she clicked something on her computer screen and looked back at me.

"I have some time I can squeeze you into my schedule for this afternoon. I usually don't have someone come in this far along, without an initial consultation, but I'll make an exception for you today. Just give me a couple minutes and we will get you taken care of and on your way in no time." She got up and walked out of the office leaving me with my sweaty hands.

Although she said she could help me, I felt no relief. I knew that my life would never be the same. I kept reminding myself that no matter what decision I made, my life was going to be altered forever and this would be the best choice. So I closed my eyes and put myself on auto-pilot, pushing down my feelings and numbing myself to anything that would cause any guilt or remorse. I dutifully followed the nurse into the examination room, answered the questions, filled out the paperwork and put on the backless gown she gave me. She directed me to put my feet in the stirrups and wait for the doctor to come back in. I closed my eyes and focused on the next day, my future and how everything would be better if I could just get through this one moment. I just kept repeating in my head, "Get through this day. Get through this day. It will all be okay. It will all be okay."

Dr. Woodren came into the room and asked me to scooch closer to the edge of the table. She pulled back my gown and I was exposed. I felt my neck and face turn red and kept wiping my palms on my gown. I swallowed back some vomit and held my jaw shut tight. God couldn't see me, could he? I mean, I haven't talked to Him in months and He felt so far away. In church, during worship, I was only lip syncing the words. He couldn't surely be looking down on me. His back was turned on me, in this moment especially, when He knew what I was doing. But it was to honor my parents and He must understand that. So, in this moment, I knew I was hidden from everyone and my secret was mine to keep. Except for this doctor and nurse and the bright lights exposing my inner deceit, shining a light on my darkest secret.

I felt something metal and cold inserted into me and then I felt aching and cramping. I closed my eyes and pretended I was somewhere else. The doctor had me wait in the room for a couple hours and then she came back in and examined me again and told me I was good to go home and everything was done. There would just be some discomfort for the day and I should expect some small clots to pass later that evening. I will be back to normal in a few days. The nurse gave me some papers, ibuprofen and assured me there was nothing to worry about for the payment. They used funding from donors. Everything was paid for. Just like that I was on my way out of the office.

I got back into my car and stared at the money. I crumpled it up and shoved it into the bottom of my purse. I arrived home at the same time I normally would, like it was just a normal day and I would have been going through my usual routine at school. Today was anything but normal. I went upstairs in my room and laid down waiting for the cramping in my stomach to stop.

Later, when my mother came to get me for dinner, all I had to say to get her to leave was, "I have cramps and feel tired."

She replied with, "Oh, I'll tell everyone you're not feeling well and we will hopefully see you at breakfast."

With that, she shut the door and left me in the darkness again. I fitfully fell asleep and woke in the middle of the night to use the bathroom. When I turned the light on, I pulled my pants down to use the toilet. I felt it before I saw the blood. It was a warm sensation running down my thigh, and I didn't have to look to know what was happening. This was my punishment and I wanted it to run out of me and take my life with it...

I knew it was almost over. My ideal future was within reach. I just needed to get through this night and then I could go back to the way things were. But things would never be the same, would they? As I sat on the toilet, wallowing in my own misery, I started to get some intense cramps. After a few minutes, they started to feel better. When I looked down to see how much blood I had actually lost, my breath caught in my throat. I had to reach for the edge of the sink to steady myself. There, floating in the middle of my blood and the toilet water, was my baby.

My first reaction was shock. I thought it was just supposed to be tissue and clumps of cells. What is going on? This was not what was supposed to be inside me. It was just some parasitic sac that used my body to grow bigger. This was not supposed to be a person. Not yet! I wasn't even that far along and yet here was this little life right in front of me. I could look and see the full outline of the body and the smallest feet and hands. The whole thing was no bigger than a mouse. Horrified, I reached for the toilet handle to flush this out of my sight and mind, but no matter how much I willed my hand to move it just rested on the handle. I couldn't bear to just abandon this child even more than I already had.

A memory of my childhood came flooding back. When my brother was about 10 years old, he won a goldfish at a game during some carnival. He was so proud of his new fish and showed it to everyone triumphantly. He told everyone about his future plans for the goldfish. He was going to buy a big house with a big pond when he got old so they could be neighbors and maybe they could even swim together. Well, about 3 days after he brought the goldfish home, he found it floating in the bowl, dead. My father instructed him to flush it down the toilet and told him it wasn't a big deal because those things didn't live long anyway. I followed my brother into the bathroom and watched as he acted strong and tough like my father always did, but when he went to flush the goldfish he turned to me with tears and simply said, "I can't, please do it for me."

He then ran from the room leaving me with a floating goldfish staring up at me from the toilet. I couldn't do it either, so I scooped the goldfish up with a bath toy and sneaked it outside. I used a spoon from the kitchen to dig a small hole near the shed in the backyard where my mother had a row of hostas growing. I said a little prayer over this goldfish and thanked him for the joy he brought to my brother's life, even if only for a short period of time.

Now here I was again. I knew if I flushed this down but buried a fish I would truly be unforgivable. So I turned away and stared at myself in the mirror. Willing the inner strength I summoned earlier to turn down this deadly path to help finish the job. I took a cup that was sitting on the sink and scooped up the little form from the water and then cleaned myself and the bathroom. After I was changed, I took the cup and slowly opened the door. The lights were out and the house was quiet. Again, working in the dark, I snuck through the house, to the stairs and eventually to the sliding glass door in the kitchen. Closing it slowly behind me, I grabbed my mother's garden bag from the back porch and walked barefoot through the backyard.

The ground was cold and my feet were feeling tingly from the frost, but I didn't care. I deserved everything I got. I found my way to the same spot I used years ago and started digging at the cold, hard ground with a small shovel from the garden bag. I finally got the ground to break free and quickly dug a small hole in the dirt. I picked the cup up and slid the little body out and into the hole. I pushed some dirt over it, but not before I saw a little foot illuminated by the moonlight sticking out of the ground. I hurriedly piled more dirt over it, wishing I could do the same to my memories and black them out forever.

After I had finished, I stood up and thought I should probably say a prayer for this life at the very least. I felt like I should see this through to the end and have a proper say over this burial and perhaps I'd find some kind of closure, too. When I opened my mouth to say a prayer the only thing I could think of was an apology, "I'm sorry," I muttered. "I'm sorry, I'm sorry." By now, the tears were flowing from my eyes and I just kept apologizing. How could I bear to even think God would want to hear my prayers? Surely he must have turned away from me and wouldn't be able to watch this happen. He didn't want to hear my words. So I walked back inside. I threw the cup away not wanting to be reminded of what it held ever again.

I went back to my room and crawled into bed with dirty fingernails and wet feet. No matter how much of the blanket I pulled on top of myself, I still felt cold. My entire body was shivering. That night, sleeping through a painkiller haze, I dreamt that roots started slithering into my room and under the slit of light at the bottom of my bedroom door. As I lay in bed, they slowly made their way up the side of my comforter and the end of the dirty roots held me down. I couldn't move. When I went to scream, they covered my mouth. I noticed that the end of the roots were little hands and they weren't leaving behind a trail of dirt on my blankets. They were trailing blood.

My eyes flew open. It felt like there was some unseen force in the room that was literally pushing down on my body and it was an effort to inhale a breath of air. I reached up to my face and pulled my hands away. They were wet and I realized I had been crying. Who were these tears for? Me or my child? I laid in bed for the rest of the night staring at the sliver of light under my door. I stared at it until it blended in with the light shining from my windows and the two were no longer discernible.

The next morning, when the sun came up, the house smelled like bacon as my mother cooked breakfast for my father. I could hear my sister rummaging through her closet in the room adjacent to mine. I looked around, surprised that life went on. It felt like I was part of some alternate reality where I went through such a traumatic experience but everyone else walked around like everything was totally normal without a care in the world. I pulled my knees to my chest as I closed my eyes and tried to calm my racing thoughts and heart. I can do this, one day at a time. That was the only way to get through this. I needed to lay down layers of time to make this disappear. I've heard some people say that time heals all wounds. Can the same be said for time concealing wounds? By keeping busy, I can put enough time between what happened and the present that I won't even remember what I did. I can bury it so deep inside of me that not even an atomic bomb could shake it from my subconscious. Maybe if I pursued a degree in nursing, like my mother, I could reason with myself that by helping others it would balance out the horrible act I committed and everything would be okay.

So that's what I did from that point on. I spent the rest of the school year studying hard and picked up an after-school job at the local grocery store stacking shelves. I ignored the phone calls from friends until finally they stopped trying. Tina eventually gave up too and she soon had a boyfriend who she devoted all her time to. I volunteered for any and all activities at my church and within our community. My parents beamed at my selflessness; if they only knew just how selfish I really was. Through the summer, I worked two jobs and had my bags packed for college weeks before it was time to leave.

When college started up in the fall my incredible work ethic pretty much stayed the same. I was completely devoted to my studies and working at the library. I even picked up shifts at the nursing home outside of town during breaks and summer vacations. By the time I graduated, I had worked meticulously at my schedule so that nothing out of the ordinary happened. I was always busy, with either work or studies, so I didn't have time to think about anything else. The days passed without any marked difference and I had earned a reputation of being a hard, tireless worker. Needless to say, I graduated with honors and for the first time in a long time, I felt that I could breathe a sigh of relief. I was well on my way to start helping others and making up for my past sins. I was ready to find a sense of forgiveness – from God or myself, I couldn't tell.

I decided to work as an in-home nurse for elderly individuals. I balanced my schedule by also working at local nursing homes. I found a great agency to work for in Cincinnati, which was about three hours from my hometown. I felt like this was a fresh start. Plus, the job would enable me to work with older individuals and greatly reduce my chance of having to help with young children or worse the maternity ward in a hospital. I remember doing a training in college in which we had to gain experience by assisting expecting mothers and newborn care. It was the hardest time of my college career. There was even one day when I had a panic attack and had to hide from the other nursing students, in a supply closet, in the hospital. I hid in a dark corner, in the back, behind boxes of gauze and plastic gloves, and tried to calm my heart and breathing for almost two hours.

For the next couple years, I was finding a steady rhythm in my life, the days passed seamlessly. When I had time off, I would sit at home and read lengthy novels. I was quickly becoming a valuable employee through the agency and was gaining trust with my patients. One of my favorite patients was a man named Phillip. He regularly flew to Florida to visit his daughter and was gone for weeks at a time. Before he left on one of his trips he asked me to house sit for him and even though my agency would frown on this, I obliged.

I found being at his home, alone in the woods, made me calmer. It had to be a combination of being completely disconnected from cell phone service, the breathtaking views of the forest through his floor-to-ceiling windows and being surrounded by nature. This truly seemed to be a place where I could find peace. Maybe it was because I just had time to spend in his awesome nature getaway, in the woods, that I let my guard down slightly. When I bumped into a past high school acquaintance, I actually said yes to a coffee when he asked me out. Maybe I was also feeling lonely on my self-made island for one. I needed to find comfort and I was yearning for someone to connect with.

Tim wasn't anything special. He was about my height and had a medium build. He was always casual in jeans, a t-shirt and scuffed sneakers. I found him to be very non-threatening and when he told me he delivered pizzas and lived with a group of guys next to the local cinema, I couldn't believe that this man was still living the same life as he probably did when he moved here after high school, seven years ago. We stayed in touch and I found myself looking forward to our casual dates. It just seemed easy with him. He loved to play video games and would often talk about his fantasy quests through a game and laugh about some funny delivery stories from work. He was never pushy and it just felt natural.

I surprised myself by asking him to move in with me after we had been seeing each for several months. I was even more surprised when he said yes. Eventually, we decided to get married and there was a huge celebration back home. Our parents had known each other through church and were delighted that their children found each other in the big city and it was "destiny". His parents were delighted with my successful career and hoped my work ethic would wear off on him. My parents were relieved that I had finally found a man and they could stop asking if there was anybody special in my life. It was bad enough that my brother and sister had already got married and my mother and father talked about them incessantly, which served as some sort of reminder of my own relationship failures.

This felt like the next step and I needed to be able to focus on it. Besides, Tim was harmless and he didn't even expect anything out of me. The sex wasnt even a big deal to him. I had shared on our wedding night that I had a bad experience in high school that I wasnt ready to elaborate on, but sex was very uncomfortable for me. He said we could take our time and when I was ready he would be there. I was only able to have intercourse if we had gone out and I made myself very drunk. I suspected that when I worked and he was home, in the afternoons, he watched a lot of porn. Some women would be annoyed by this habit but I didn't care as long as he didnt come to me for his needs. I think we were both with each other as sort of a peace offering to our parents to stop nagging and just let us live, to find some breathing room.

Marriage was a welcome addition to the life I was building for myself. Everyday when I went to bed I felt more at ease and the past was long behind me. Tim and I were enjoying our quiet life we had built together. We decided to go out for the evening and celebrate my 30th birthday. I chose a local Italian restaurant known for its manicotti. Tim, of course, ordered the usual chicken strips and fries. He even ate like a teenager. He was probably looking forward to me getting tipsy because I was well on my way to my third glass of wine before we even finished eating. I didn't mind anyway.

What he wasn't aware of was that I was not only using Alcohol as a way to deal with having sex with him, but I also found it easier to get a better nights sleep after drinking. When I would get home in the evening from a shift and he was still out delivering I would often drink by myself because I found it was one of the easiest ways to help cope with my insomnia. There was no way I would get a prescription for this. I did not want anybody to think I was having any problems. Everything was going great for me and I had meticulously set up this careful life. Little did I know that what I thought was a well-built life constructed on level ground was actually built on a cliff's edge and a storm was coming. Would I be able to withstand the storms of my past colliding with my future?

PRECONCEPTION CARE

Elena

Sunlight poured through my windshield. I had to put my arm up to shield my eyes and be able to see the road. The voice from my phone said I had arrived at my destination. I pulled up to a small yellow duplex. The house was perfectly symmetrical. I could imagine slicing it right down the middle like those exercises in elementary school where you had to find the point of symmetry. Both sides, of the duplex, had a door on the porch and a window next to the door with white shutters. I couldn't discern anything different between the two sides and I wondered if the place on the left was rented out too.

I walked around to the passenger side and tucked my unruly, brown, curly hair behind my ears as I settled a box on my hip. As I approached my new place, I reached into my purse, which was hanging from my shoulder, to fish out the keys I picked up from the real estate agency a few hours ago. Walking up to the front door, I was already thinking about how I could start decorating with some cute plants. My thoughts were interrupted when I noticed the key wouldn't turn in the lock. I made a face, annoyed that this was the way my new start was going. I fought off worries and put the keys back in my purse.

The door abruptly swung open and a woman faced me in blue hospital scrubs. She had her brown hair pulled back in a bun and looked to be about my age, maybe a little younger. I smiled at my mistake and quickly introduced myself, "Hello, I'm Elena, I just moved into this duplex and I've found out that I'm at the wrong place. Thanks for helping me out already!"

The person on the other side of the door stood there; quietly assessing me. She let me stand there for a couple awkward seconds. Just when I began to think she was going to slam the door in my face, she blinked and smiled slightly.

She introduced herself, "Hello, I'm Darcy. My husband, Tim, and I live here. We were wondering who was going to replace Nico. He used to be part of a band. It was always so annoying listening to his same, boring playlists over and over again. It's not like these walls are that thick."

She started walking back into her house, which I took as some informal invitation. I hesitantly followed her in, with my box still on my hip.

Darcy walked to her counter and filled up a glass with wine and held it up to me with questioning eyes "I was just making myself a drink, would you like one?"

"No, I'm good, still got some unpacking to do tonight, but I would love to have one another night."

She put the glass down and threw her hands up, "I'm so sorry, here let me help you with your stuff." Reaching out, she took the box and motioned for me to go back out to the porch. "Let me help you with anything else you have. Sorry about that. I was just getting off from a long shift and feeling a little spacey from being tired. I am happy to help."

I thanked her as we started carrying the rest of the boxes in from my car. She was probably tired, I knew nurses sometimes worked long hours so that's why I decided to brush off my strange feelings. She was probably overworked. I shouldn't judge her for being a little hmm, should I say odd. But who was I to judge? Wasn't I weird too? Aren't we all at times. As I unpacked some stuff on the kitchen counter, she looked around the living room, remarking on how disorientating it was because it was the same set up as her house. Except everything was set up on the left side in her place.

She had her hands on her hips and stood there for a couple seconds, we both didn't really know what to say so I broke the silence, "Hey, you hungry? I'm starved and I bet you are too. Maybe you could start me off right by showing me a great place to eat."

She went to open her mouth and say something but then quickly closed it and looked towards the front door. Then she turned back to me and slowly started to shake her head up and down, "You know what, that would be nice. I know a great Thai place that serves the best Pad See Ew."

As I closed the door and locked it, I smiled a little to myself. *See I'm already making friends! This is going to be great!*

Darcy

The light from the refrigerator lit up the dark kitchen momentarily while I pulled out my bottle of wine. Most nights, when Tim worked, I didn't even bother to eat and just stuck to a liquid diet. Not even bothering to change, I stood there in my blue scrubs as I took that first satisfying drink of the day. I felt it rush down me and the familiar pull of the alcohol relaxing me. I could feel my body and my racing thoughts calm down. Sometimes, when I was feeling particularly jittery, I would even add some Vodka to the glass. As I stood in the cool, dark room, ready to pour my next glass, I could hear the sound of keys being inserted in the front lock. Standing still, I listened further, assuming it was Tim home early. He was probably trying to use his work key on the front door, again, ugh… he was so clueless sometimes. Annoyed that he was ruining my usual wind down time, I walked with a scowl on my face, to the front door, unlocking it and swinging it open.

I was immediately surprised to see a young woman standing there. She was about my age with brown, bouncy curls spilling around her shoulders. She had a box on her hip and a look of surprise on her face, too. It took me a second to figure out she was most likely the new tenant next door. We probably came to that conclusion at the same time, because she raised her hand and introduced herself as Elena, the new tenant next door. Still reeling from the large glass of wine and change in my evening schedule, I stared at her hand like she was a mirage. If I reached out to shake it, would it make her real?

Snapping out of my thoughts, I responded, "Hello, I'm Darcy. My husband, Tim, and I live here. We were wondering who was going to replace Nico. He used to be part of a band and it was always so annoying listening to his same, boring playlists over and over again. It's not like these walls are that thick." That idiot musician next door finally moved out. I couldn't stand him or his mopey friends. They were always loitering on the front porch, smoking joints, and talking about climate change. His music was so slow and depressing. The melody seeped into my bones at night, pulling me into a foggy deep sleep, in which my dreams always seemed to be an old black and white noir film.

Without even realizing it, I walked back to the counter and started pouring another glass of wine. Lost in my thoughts and old habits, I realized Elena had followed me in. I decided to offer her a glass of wine. She declined and stood there, with a cardboard box perched on her hip, labeled Special Stuff.

I was immediately curious. What could be so special that it would deserve its own box and label? I didn't bring anything with me when I moved in. Preferring the bland beige decor the place was already furnished with. I brought nothing of significance from home with me. I was acting like a weirdo. I realized I should probably make an effort if we were to live next to each other. I offered to help with the boxes from the car she gladly accepted. She flashed a big, white smile at me.

I noticed she had dimples on both cheeks and she had an inviting personality. I felt like I had stepped out of the cold. Being near her was like standing in the sun or near a warm fire. For some reason, I felt drawn to her. I carried a box, from the back seat of her car, labeled Bathroom Crap, and placed it on the armchair in the living room.

I looked around and noted how strange it was to be standing in her duplex, which looked exactly the same as mine, but somehow flipped. Even the furniture was the same. The only noticeable difference I could see was the color of the kitchen cabinets. Maybe the paint was on sale that day in algae green.

Elena broke into that bright smile and asked, "Hey, you hungry? I'm starved and I bet you are too. Maybe you could start me off right by showing me a great place to eat."

I looked toward the door and thought of a million excuses to say no, stay in my bubble, keep focused on my future and my goals. But for some reason I can't even fathom, I looked back and agreed. I should have known that leaving my rational, disciplined plans, and going out of character would only lead to death. As she turned on the front porch and slid the lock into place it was almost as if our paths were locking into place too, we were on the same path now. A slippery downhill slope, careening into one pileup of carefully laid plans and broken glass shards of emotions and guilt.

Elena

The next couple of months went by fast. Soon, spring had shifted into a humid summer, slowing all activity down and seemingly melting the resolve in Darcy to avoid me. I wasn't sure how to take her at first. I made it a mission to be friends and make the most out of every relationship I had in my life. This was part of my goal to be a new and improved Elena.

Every aspect of my new life seemed to be falling into place. Darcy helped me find a job at an outpatient mental health center in town. Bright Paths was looking for an office manager. Darcy talked to one of the therapists there and I started within a week of moving to town. Most of my tasks centered around scheduling for patients and their therapists, doing insurance verifications and submitting payments to insurance carriers. I was thrilled because my funds would only have lasted about five months, if I hadn't found steady income. The job was not only fulfilling monetarily, but I also really enjoyed working in an environment where I felt I was making a difference. It was such a stark difference compared to my previous job. Here, people left with hope. In my past job, we ripped hope from people. It was something I rarely let myself remember. Being here and making a difference in people's lives would start making up for my past mistakes.

To repay Darcy for my newly found employment, I took her out for a night on the town. We settled on a local place named Dave's Dive Bar, which had a live band for the night. I noticed she didn't take long to find a bartender and order a couple shots. Pretty soon we had a table near the front where we could enjoy the band and relax from our long week. I can feel the effects of the alcohol and any apprehensions I had melted away. I bounce my head to the music and tap my foot to the rhythm. Darcy sits up straight, holding her drink in both hands on the table, almost like she is afraid someone is going to take it from her.

A man in a white button up asks me to dance. I look at Darcy and she just purses her lips in indifference. I take his hand and pretty soon I'm doing my best drunk dance moves. My hands are in the air and I'm shaking my curls like I'm a professional 80's rock star. My dance partner laughs as he tries his best. I put my arm around his shoulder and throw some of my long locks over the top of his head to help. We both throw back our heads and laugh at his makeshift wig.

After the song, he offers to buy us a drink and Darcy gives him a cold look, "We can take care of our own drinks, thank you very much though."

He doesn't say anything but tips his head to me and wanders back to his group. I don't say anything to her about the abruptness. This is one of the reasons I wanted to take her out. I hope that one day I can break through the cold barrier she has put up in front of herself. Coming out tonight is a start.

Darcy

It's turning out to be a nice change having Elena around. Our shared front porch is always neat and tidy. Which is a nice change from constantly sweeping ashes off from the last guy. She has started putting planters on her side and the flowers are soon overflowing, hanging off the side and adding smacks of color that I can't help but be drawn to. Sometimes, I reach out my hand as I walk past them to feel the silky petals. Being around her is like going outside after a long, dark winter. I'm slowly shedding my layers and shaking the frost from my cold limbs. Her energy is often contagious. I never would have imagined doing things like: checking out the local artist celebration for no reason except to have fun. Elena encouraged me to do things like that.

Maybe I was lonely. Tina used to be one of my best friends in high school. We would sneak secretive glances to each other and giggle over boys. We even would raid each other's closets. At some point though, both of those girls I remember from my childhood became strangers to me. One left behind in a small town and one left behind in a cornfield.

It was nice to be able to share things with someone else again. Hanging out with Elena was effortless. She went out of her way for everyone we met. She regularly would give out compliments to people in front of us at the cash register – remarking on earrings or their sneakers. It was like life was slowly coming into focus for me and I realized there were other people around me too. My normal routine would go something like this: get up, go to work and take care of my patients. In a way it was like I was just ticking boxes off on a to do list. There was no real affection there.

Tim was just there too. Taking care of himself and hanging out with his friends. His low maintenance lifestyle didn't beg for too much attention from me. Plus his mother called him everyday and babied over him so much he probably got all the love and nurturing he needed from her. When I would get home from work, it would bring a smile to my face to see Elena, with her big smile, waving from the porch where she would be tending to her plants or reading a book.

One afternoon, we were enjoying each other's company while sitting on the front porch. Elena was browsing the local job listings on her laptop.

I inquired about her job search. "Hey, any good jobs on there?"

Elena sighed and closed her laptop, "Nothing really."

I decided to tell her about a possible job, "I have a patient that mentioned having trouble getting into her therapist because they don't have an office manager. She was just venting to me about the situation, but I could see what office she goes to and call them on your behalf. Maybe that could work out for you?"

Her beaming smile broke out, "That would be awesome! In my prior job, I was actually an office manager." She was looking down now focusing on some curls as she twirled them between her fingers, possibly looking for split ends.

I sensed there was something there she was holding back, "Where did you say you moved from again?"

Letting go of her hair and resting back on her elbows she gave me a half smile, "I travel where the wind takes me. I used to be in a place where I didn't find joy in anything I was doing. I needed a fresh start so here I am. Maybe I'll find something here I've been missing. It's not like I have any real family. I was raised by my grandmother, in Texas, and there isn't anybody else in my life. But, hey, I got some great new friends here like you now! So let's not sit here and focus on yucky stuff like the past. Let's go get ice cream! It's finally getting warm out."

So that was that. We really didn't talk much about her past after our brief conversation on the porch. Why would I pry though, wasn't I also trying to bury my past and focus on my future?

After a couple weeks working at her new job Elena texts me on a Friday.

HEY GIRL!! I am so glad you got me this job. I love working here and the people are great. Even the clients are great. Plus, they even let me bring in some plants. It really livens the place up… LOL…

You know me and my plant obsession…Anyways, to repay you and your act of kindness, I want you to get dressed up and be ready at 8 tonight. We are going out! XOXO seeya later.

> Hey, It was no problem! I'm glad everything is working out for you there. I haven't gone out in forever! A little nervous but I guess you won't take no for an answer. I'll see you later.

Throwing open my closet door, when I got home, I'm surprised to see that over the years, I've actually turned into a cartoon character in regards to wardrobe. I could wear the same outfit everyday and it would be the "Darcy outfit". Almost half of my clothes are hospital scrubs. The other half consist of jeggings and shirts or sweatshirts. Most of them are similar in style and color. I really don't dress up when Tim and I go out. It's been a very long time since I've gone out with a friend. Ultimately, I decide on a plain, white shirt and my newest jeggings.

When I answer the door, Elena is exactly as I would have expected. Her brown, curly hair spilled down her back. Big, golden hoops and a black dress with sequins down the sides. When she comes into my house, the lamp from the living room catches on her dress and sends tiny shimmers of light dancing across the wall. We couldn't be more different, but here we are, going out on the town. After we decide on which place to go, I immediately head to the bar. Even with the glass of wine I downed before we came, I know I'm going to need more to get through this night.

I ask for a cranberry and vodka. Thinking about it again, I tell the bartender to make it a double. I get the same for Elena and walk them to our table, which is located near the front of the bar. It's loud and everything seems sticky. I sit forward in my seat and hold my drink listening to the band's remake of 80s rock and roll greats. After just one drink, Elena is shaking her head and getting really into the music. She is singing along with the musician and doing an air guitar. I can't believe she is like that after only one drink! I'm glad I came out tonight because she really needs someone to keep an eye out for her and make sure she doesnt do anything stupid. If I'm to be a good friend, I want to make sure she doesn't make the same mistakes I did. I'll have to stay close to her.

A group of guys, on the other side of the bar, motion to us and I see a man in a white button up start walking over. His buddies behind him egg him on as he looks back at them. Ugh, his buttons are completely messed up. They aren't even lined up correctly. If Tim wore button down shirts, this is probably how he would be dressed. I shudder at the thought of my husband.

When he reaches our table, a lot of the bravado he had, is now gone. Without his friends beside him, he shyly asks Elena if she wants to dance. Throwing back the contents of her drink, she puts the glass on the table and flashes me a big smile. If she is asking for my permission, I won't give it. I also don't want to be the reason our night is boring so I just give a look of indifference. She takes his hand and they go to the dance floor.

Watching them, out there, makes me feel so enraged. How can she just act like that?! Dancing and being so close to him... doesn't she know what kind of trouble she could find herself in? He could be ready to put drugs in her drink and she would be finding herself in the back of a van somewhere dead. I root myself to the seat and watch their every move. I didn't even get something else to drink when my own cup became empty.

After the song is over, they make their way back to the table. The man puts his hands in his jeans pockets, "Would you ladies like a refill on drinks?"

I sit forward and look him in the eyes, not able to help myself when I let my abhorrence out, "We can take care of our own drinks, thank you very much though."

With that he puts up his hands in surrender and turns and walks back to his friends. If I was too hostile in my response, Elena doesn't say anything. After that, we watched the show for a little bit and left about an hour later.

On the porch, Elena hugs me and thanks me for the night out, "It was fun tonight! Sorry if I get a little wild. I can't handle my alcohol very well. You sure do keep an eye on me. Thanks, Darcy."

Once she lets me go, we both go inside. I find myself smiling. See, I was doing the right thing. We are looking out for each other.

Elena

One weekend, I stopped over around lunch time, to see if Darcy wanted to check out the local Farmers Market, on the south side of town. Her husband, Tim, answered the door. I guess when you visualize people and then meet them and they are 100% different from what you imagined, you find yourself at a loss. I had built him up in my head as someone tall, thin, wearing suspenders and reading glasses. Just as serious and socially distant as Darcy. Here, in front of me, though, was just the opposite. Tim was wearing light jeans, scruffy sneakers and a Shirt that read, *Pizza is always the answer*. His sandy hair was sticking up slightly in the back and he had a game controller in one hand.

Reaching out my hand I introduce myself, " Hey, I'm Elena, from next door. I was looking for Darcy."

As I said this, he broke into a smile and stepped forward. With my hand still awkwardly extended, he pulled me in for a big hug.

"I'm so glad to finally meet you!" He beamed at me, "I always tell Darcy she works too much and needs to get out more. With my work, as a delivery driver, I don't get to see her most evenings. It made me feel really good when Darcy told me you two met and had been going out. She hasn't made that many friends around here. I'm so glad you guys have hit it off."

I can't help but feel just as happy as he is so I smile back, "I was actually looking to go to the farmers market and was hoping she was around to come with me."

He steps back into the house and extends a hand to the armchair next to the couch. "Well, she actually is house sitting for one of her patients outside of town. Some guy named Phillip who she has been helping for years. The cell service is very crappy out there. I doubt she would get a text. You're welcome to hang out with me for the afternoon. I actually had a buddy cancel on me and I could really use some back up for this next level." He reaches down and offers me a game controller.

I sit down on the chair and pull my legs up to sit cross legged. I take the controller from his hand. "Let's do this!"

The next weekend there is a block party in the neighborhood. The smell of burgers grilling and fresh cut grass fill the air. Someone hired a live band and notes of 70s rock music float through my brain waves like an inner tube down a lazy river. I'm feeling happy. Like my life is lining up to what I had wanted. The street is closed off and there are makeshift tables of all sizes and folding chairs fill the street. As it starts to get darker and everyone's bellies are full, people begin to divide into smaller groups.

Darcy, Tim and I find ourselves hanging around a place about three houses down from us with a few other couples. Tim was talking about his grass and how he was trying to get perfect zig-zag stripes on the front lawn and asked if anyone would be interested in him practicing on their yards.

The blonde sitting next to him raised her hand, "Maybe you could mow off whatever animals keep eating off my hostas. No matter what I do, they keep getting nibbled. I'll take the little varmint bodies and bury them in the soil. Then my Hostas can live off them. Ha!" She slaps her knee and takes another swig of her beer.

Tim goes to respond but I can't hear him, my focus elsewhere now. Out of the corner of my eye, I see Darcy straighten up. Her free hand that isn't holding a wine cooler, makes a slow fist. Her knuckles are turning white. It seems that her whole body is tight. Her face is expressionless. There is something robotic to her right now. Like she is putting herself on autopilot.

Was it the crack about the animals? I never took Darcy for an animal lover. Earlier, when a dog came over with a stick hanging out of its

Darcy

During the end of June, as I'm driving out to meet one of my favorite clients, Phillip, I choose to call my mom back. I know my call will not last long due to the spotty service. In fact, this is usually when I try to call her back, knowing I wont be stuck talking for hours about how well my sister is doing. She is married to a man that just got his medical degree and they plan on building their own home. If she isnt talking about my sister, then she talks about my brother and his students in his music class. It's all I can do to keep the car on the road as I lose myself in other thoughts to drone out her incessant praises of my siblings and their perfect lives. I find myself wondering if she ever brings me up to her friends? I mean, I'm married and work hard too. Does that count for anything brag worthy?

Maybe she is still upset about the time Tim and I came home for Thanksgiving. He tried too hard to please my parents. He grabbed the corner of the table cloth with his napkin and when he went to stand he inadvertently caused the gravy boat to tip and spill hot, dark gravy all over my mothers perfect set up. We all ate our food standing at the counter, in the kitchen, while my mother scrubbed the tablecloth and floor in the dining room. Yeah, needless to say, that's one of the reasons I avoid going home. Even though I got married, I might as well not have, because my mother thinks Tim is just a waste of space. In a way, she is kinda right about that. He isn't all that bad though. He does try and even on my most challenging days he tends to make me feel better.

While my mother is droning on about the fundraiser her church is putting on this July, I reflect back on a particularly rough night this past January. I have the hardest time during winter. Not because of the usual lack of vitamin D, or so called seasonal affective disorder… blah blah, but because my subconscious reminds me of that night. The nightmares come rearing their ugly heads, tipping the iceberg of my subconscious upside down and forcing me to see my true self.

On one of those nights, I woke up in a cold sweat and swiped my face as the tears came. Tim reached over and started rubbing my back. After I was calm, he pulled me into an embrace and shared with me that his sister used to have night terrors when he was little. She would come into his room at night to calm down. He would read her stories under the blanket, with his lantern. She would fall asleep on his lap with visions of fairy princesses and magical bunnies; instead of the dark monsters swimming through her thoughts previously. It was this caring and thoughtful side that ultimately made me forgive all his silly and immature acts that would leave other wives screaming and throwing game systems out the window. I guess it just worked for us.

Finally, I crested a hill and my mothers voice started to cut out, "Mom, oops I'm starting to lose service, I'll have to call you back. Good luck this month at your fundraiser."

Call failed flashed on my screen. Ahh blissful quiet for the rest of the 20 minute drive. I pulled up to the house, snuggly nestled between the trees. A nature oasis as Phillip called it. He told his adult children that he would be living here until he died, whether they liked it or not. They were the ones who set me up to come and help him. He was one of my first patients as an in-home nurse.

Like most of my other patients, I checked his vitals, went over medications and helped make sure he had transportation lined up for upcoming appointments and wellness checks. I almost always stayed with him longer than other appointments. Phillip loved to walk me around his ever-growing vegetable and flower garden, which he still tended for his wife, even though she passed away more than 15 years ago. We would talk about funny anecdotes from other appointments I had with clients and have solid discussions on politics and economics. Not that I was invested in the news. He always liked to have a "good debate" on current events.

On my recent visit, while I was taking his blood pressure, the offer on watching his house came up, "I'm going to be gone next weekend and wanted to know if you could stop over and check in on things. Maybe watch over the garden if it gets too hot?"

I recorded my findings on his blood pressure before responding. "Sure, how about Saturday I come over for the day. I think I'll head home before it gets dark though. I've met a new friend that just moved in next door. She is adjusting to being new in town. I would hate for her to go out on her own and run into trouble."

He took his hand and placed it gingerly over mine. "That would be marvelous, my dear."

Growing up, I never had a grandfather figure in my life. If I had, I would have wanted him to be just like Phillip. Usually home health nurses don't have relationships with their patients like this, as it would be a conflict of interest, but what my agency didn't know wouldn't hurt them. Besides, what would they do, fire me? I was one of their most reliable, hard-working nurses. I was an asset to the company. I kept my head down and minded my own business. If they knew I house sat for Phillip, I doubt anybody would say anything.

After I got back from the house sitting that Saturday, I saw the lights on in the living room. I walked into the house and I found Tim and Elena, with pizza and soda, on the coffee table. They are both laughing and shouting, at the tv, as a broadcaster delivers a play-by-play, on the sports game they are watching.

Tim stands to greet me, "Hey! Look who I found," as he points his arms to Elena, as if presenting me with a gift.

She stands up and I notice some crumbs fall from her lap, onto the floor, and I make a mental note to vacuum later. "Hey, girl! I stopped by earlier to take you to the farmers market and get some fresh veggies, but I ran into this goofball." She sticks a thumb in Tim's direction as he smiles. "Well, now I can add gamer to my resume, if I ever lose my job as an office manager."

She gives me a hug and I put the effort into returning the act. "Well, I'm glad you guys got to meet. It looks like you had a fun day. I'll be right back. I'm going to put my stuff away."

I walked to the coat closet and put my boots away that I used for walking in the garden. I noticed my left hand has dirt around the fingernails. My chest feels tight and I hurriedly start walking back to the bathroom in my bedroom. Tim and Elena have their backs to me now shouting at the referee again. I flip on the lights and silently curse myself. This must have happened earlier, after I took off my gloves and walked back to the house. I accidentally stepped on one of the cucumber plants and I bent down to fix it by pushing some of the dirt over. I was focused on my schedule for the upcoming week and wasn't paying attention to what I was doing. I hated when my fingernails were dirty. I hated anything that reminded me of that night.

I poured some bleach into the water I had sitting in the sink and grabbed a new toothbrush and began scrubbing my fingernails until they were clean. I could feel the tightness in my chest start to subside. I drained the water and cleaned everything up before I went back out.

Tim made a funny face as he sniffed the air, "You clean his house today too? I smell bleach on you."

As I started clearing some of the mess from the coffee table, Elena stood and helped carry some chip bowls into the kitchen.

"Hey, Tim was saying there is a neighborhood block party next weekend. It sounds like fun! Do you want to cook up something with me that we can bring?"

Ugh. I forgot that was coming up. that stupid block party has been happening every year since I've lived here. Tim has always gone alone. I've ensured my schedule was full so I could conveniently be absent during the festivities. Maybe this year will be different.

"You know what? Sure. Let's make something. How about cookies?"

From the living room, I noticed Tim raise his eyebrows and a smile started to play on his lips. He acted like he wasn't paying attention to our conversation, but I just ignored him.

Elena was smiling now and excitedly throwing ideas out, "Great! How about we try conchas? I haven't made them in a long time. My Grandmother would make them from scratch and it would be nice to share that recipe with you. I think you will love them. Plus, I bet no one else will have them at the party. Ooh… let's also get our nails done! We can have little fireworks on them for July?"

I looked down at my nails. They sparkled from their recent scrub, "Sure. That actually sounds like fun."

On the following Friday, I took a personal day to help Elena bake. It was my first planned day off, ever, I think. Typically, my personal time just gets wasted each year. This might be another first for me, baking in my kitchen. The smell of warm, sugary dough fills the air. Elena was kneading more dough while she was sharing tips from her grandmother.

"We made these about once a month. My grandmother was born in a little village in Mexico and she insisted we never lose our traditions. She used to call me her little sombra. That means shadow. We would sit down to make them and she would tell me little stories about my mother as a child. That was the only time she would talk about her. I don't know if I looked forward to the times when she made conchas because they were delicious or because I got to hear about my mother."

She lifted an arm up and used the back of her wrist to wipe at her head, accidentally leaving a bit of flour on her forehead.

While I was measuring some ingredients for her into another bowl, I took my chance to ask about her mother. "Did you ever reunite with your mother, or is she still out of the picture?"

Pausing for just a second I could see Elena gathering her thoughts, "My mother died when I was just a baby. She had worked to be very successful in her career and by the time she was 40 she still hadn't been married. According to my grandmother, she wanted a baby more than anything so she tried In Vitro Fertilization. It was successful. I guess I have a father out there somewhere. She used an anonymous donor so... Anyways, she developed high blood pressure when she was pregnant with me and the doctor suggested my mother not go through with the pregnancy. She said she would rather die than end the pregnancy. In the end, that's what happened. My grandmother was close to 60 by then. She stepped up to the plate and raised me."

Now I felt bad about asking, this was such a personal story, "Is your grandmother still in Texas?"

Elena stopped kneading momentarily, as if thinking of a sweet memory. She started again with a sad smile, "No, she passed when I was just about to start college. She was one of the most caring people I've ever met. Sometime along my way I lost some of what she taught me. That's part of the reason I moved here and decided to start over. I want to make her proud of me." Elena smiled up at me, her eyes misty, "What about you, you never mention your family."

I rolled my eyes, "Because there is nothing to tell, I'm not close to them. I always feel like I'm never good enough for them. Especially my mom. So I just do my own thing."

Elena didn't respond and I was surprised at myself for being so honest with her. I don't think I've ever shared that with anyone. But then again, it felt like this was a raw, emotional time for both of us. I might as well get it off my chest.

Elena was shaping the dough into a ball so it could rest in the oven, when she said, "Well, I'm still glad for them. You know, mothers. Without them we wouldn't have life and plants and these yummy conchas and we wouldn't have men."

The last part she said while winking at me and giggling. Rolling my eyes at her, I

couldn't help but laugh, as she started shaking her hips and acting goofy.

She put the dough ball into the oven and grabbed a towel to wipe her hands. She looked at me, "I wouldn't be too hard on yourself, Darcy. Your family loves you. I think one day you will come to realize that." She bumped her hip into mine lightly and I smiled at her. "Alright, let's get some drinks while we wait. We can start pregaming a day early."

I grabbed my purse from its hook and looked back and agreed, "Now you're talking. I'll drive and you buy."

The following morning, I was secretly hoping for rain. The sun came out full force and people started setting up even before I was out of bed. Ugh. I guess I would have to do this after all. The silver lining: I would have two social butterflies around me to do most of the talking. Elena and Tim were both chatty enough. I likely won't need to talk at all.

Having something to drink, for most of the day, did seem to help. I hated to admit that I was slightly overwhelmed with all the people and noise from the day. I was glad when it started to quiet down and we found ourselves in a smaller group. We were sitting at a picnic table with a couple neighbors from our street. I don't remember their names. Tim had started a conversation about his favorite baseball team. Then someone complimented Elena on her nails and now she was in a deep conversation about curly hair care with someone else. I took the time to take a deep breath and drink my wine cooler. Soon, the conversation turned to Elena's plant collection, both inside and outside. She was talking about the proper care of her Snake plant and propagating so she could share with everyone.

Tim warned, "You better not try planting anything in the front lawn, I'll mow them right off. When I get to mowing, there is no telling what I'll do. I tried mowing a lightning strike pattern on the lawn once. It looked horrible. Now I'm trying to perfect my zig-zag stripes. Anyone want to let me experiment on their lawn."

They were all laughing.

One of the women, the blond one in a too tight dress responded, "Maybe you could mow off whatever animals keep eating off my hostas. No matter what I do they keep getting nibbled. I'll take the little varmint bodies and bury them in the soil. Then my Hostas can live off them. Ha!" She slaps her knee and takes another swig of her beer.

I try to swallow and find my mouth has gone dry. My mind drifts to my backyard. My mother's hostas line both sides of the shed. Is that what is happening? Are they living off the body of my baby? I can feel my body tighten up as I try to choke down emotions. Her words float into my mind and flash before my eyes, varmint… bodies… bury… hostas…

The rest of the evening goes by and I don't say a word. Elena moved next to me before we went in for the night. She was a little tipsy, at that point.

She bumped her knee against mine, "Hey. You okay?"

I just shook my head and after everyone started heading in, I went inside and crawled into bed. I pulled the blankets over my head, clothes, shoes and all. Tim knew when I was like this to just leave me alone. He stayed out in the living room and I heard his game system turn on. The familiar music from his fantasy game coming through the crack in the door.

That night I dreamt about the Hostas. I was walking closer to the shed in the backyard and I felt like I was being watched. Turning slowly, I could see nothing for miles around. The only thing there was the shed and the hostas. Walking closer, I felt it again. I saw no one. As I got closer to the hostas, I could see something strange on the leaves of the plant. Bending down, I reached out to feel the leaves of the hosta. The ends of the hosta leaves were covered in thin black hairs on both sides. When I touched one, I realized they were eyelashes. A piece of green leaf came up slowly and an eye was staring at me.

I woke up suddenly. My hand went to my chest and held down my pounding heart. I could still hear the music from the game system and figured Tim probably fell asleep on the couch. I stood up and went to the bathroom, closing the door behind me. I slid down against the wall until I was on the floor. Putting my face into my hands, I started to cry. *Would this guilt ever go away?*

I think about how some animals migrate back to the place of their birth. Scientists are amazed at these unexplainable traits in animals. Are babies the same? Tethered to their mothers by the same unseen force. Always looking for them. Listening for them. Yearning to be close to them. What happens when that bond is severed by the hands of evil? Like a murdered person haunting the halls where they were killed, am I destined to be forever haunted by the spirit of my child? Never being able to find peace.

Elena

A buzzing noise cuts into my sleep as I rub my eyes and yawn. Rolling over to investigate the noise, I see that my cell phone is vibrating on the bedside table. I pick it up to check who is disturbing my Saturday morning. It's a little past 08:00 and Darcy has texted me.

> Sorry to wake you up. I know you love sleeping in. My schedule is packed today and I left some papers I need on the kitchen table. If I drive back home, I'll be late to my first appointment and it'll mess up my whole day. Normally, I dont forget anything, but someone I know dragged me to a wing night yesterday and got me home late…so someone other than me is responsible. HA! Please, please!! Spare key for the side door is on top of the backyard light. Just stand on tiptoes and you will feel it there.

> Just for you, Darcy… Although, now you realize you owe me dinner… ☺

Well I guess there is no arguing with her logic. We stayed out late last night. Then we stayed out even later sitting on the front porch enjoying some wine. Swinging my feet over the bed, I reached up and stretched my arms over my head. The good thing about getting up early is I can clean up the house and be done in record time. I should have time to read some of the newest romance novels I picked up last week. Yeah, this is going to be a good day. As I walk into the bathroom to brush and pee real quick, I catch sight of my hair. Yikes! My curls are over the place. I'll just have to tame them later. I pull on some black leggings and an oversized shirt that has a sasquatch and the saying *Hide and Seek World Champion.* I walk around the house to Darcy's side door and feel for the key. I hope I don't accidentally grab a spider up there too, as my hand sticks to a little bit of a leftover web. Once I have the papers, I text Darcy to let her know I'm on the way.

> I'm on my way. Tim's lucky he went home for the weekend so I had to take his place getting up early for you. It's the building next to the doughnut shop on Franklin right? Plus, I literally just jumped out of bed, can you come out to the car and grab them?

Once I'm in the car my phone vibrates again.

Ha! What, do you have crazy hair today?! Nobody is here. Just bring them in. Yeah, it's the little building next to the Doughnut place we went to a couple weeks ago. See ya soon!

Darcy took me out for doughnuts once. While we were out, she showed me the tidy little white building next door which was the office for her in-home nursing agency. It's easy enough to find. I jump out of my car and start heading toward the entrance. It's so bright. The sun is glaring right in my eyes at this angle. I forgot my sunglasses in the car. I put my arm up and squint as I round the corner of the building, taking a shortcut to get out of the sun. I walk straight through the mulch instead of the sidewalk.

In my eagerness to get out of the sun, I don't see him until it's too late. He is looking down at some paperwork and I bump right into him, causing his papers to fall.

"Shoot, I'm so sorry. Here, let me help you!" I immediately lean over and start helping him collect his papers.

When I look up and catch his eye, it's like I'm blinded all over again. I'm reminded of looking at the blue sapphire gemstones in the mall and I'm curious if he moved his eyes would they glint and sparkle too? That's when he clears his throat and red starts to spread up his cheeks. Coming back to the present, I'm suddenly very aware that not only am I so close to this gorgeous man, but I'm bending over in front of him in a loose top, with no bra. He can definitely see right down my shirt! Now I'm the one blushing too. Shoving the papers into his hands, I hurry into the building glad to feel the rush of cold air greet me and cool my hot face.

Darcy is sitting in one of the chairs, at the front desk, looking through folders.

She looks up and sees me, "Thank you so much, Elena! I have to rush but I'll talk to you later okay!"

Standing and reaching for the papers she slides them into a folder and starts walking towards the front door with me.

"Umm… so the cutest guy just left and I bumped into him and he dropped some papers. When I leaned over to help him pick them up, I think I flashed him. I thought you said no one would be here!"

I think I'm going to blush again but Darcy wrinkles her nose and makes one of her gross faces. "You must have seen one of the new traveling nurses we just hired for a while. His name is Noah. We just met. I think he is here for like 13 weeks or something. Sometimes our office has traveling nurses pick up contracts temporarily when we are understaffed or we have someone leave for an extended period of time. One of our full-time people just went out on maternity leave. He is probably just covering for her. You won't have to worry about seeing him again."

After she locks the front door we head to our cars and our separate ways for the day. Waving goodbye she gets into her car and I turn and get into mine. Exhaling, I'm feeling a little sad that I wont see this Noah again. Oh well, maybe someday I'll meet someone.

Heading back home and thinking of those eyes, I'm reminded of another mortifying thought. It's been almost eight months since I've even gone on a date, not counting sex. It's a good thing I'm taking a shower when I get back, cause I need a cold shower for sure!

As I turned the page of my romance novel, the sound of a car pulling into the shared driveway caused me to look up. Darcy was just getting back from work. She walked over to the porch and sat down opposite of me, on one of the wicker chairs I found at the flea market. It was a beautiful evening. There was a light mist of rain earlier that seemed to break up the humidity and I had been enjoying the last thralls of summer.

"How's it going buddy? Want to order some take out tonight because it's just the two of us?"

Opening her mouth to respond, we both looked up to see Tim pulling his truck into the driveway.

He stepped out with flowers in hand and a big smile. "There's my beautiful wife! I know I wasn't supposed to come back until tomorrow; however, I was with my sister and she told me happy anniversary. I felt like a complete jerk. Please forgive me! I came back as soon as she reminded me. Let me take you out tonight!"

Darcy scrunched up her face in that annoyed way. "I guess I forgot about that too. Umm… it doesn't matter."

I didn't want her to think we had to do something. Tim was standing there with flowers and being so sweet. He was even wearing a shirt with gnomes that read, *To Gnome me is to love me*. I mean, come on! This is too cute to pass up.

"Darcy, this is so sweet! Come on, I'll help you get ready. Let's get some caffeine in you and find something cute for you to wear!"

With Tim and I both smiling at her, she finally relented a little and shrugged her shoulders. "Okay. You're right. Thanks, Tim."

She got up and took the flowers and he leaned over and kissed her on the cheek. That was the first time I saw any kind of intimacy between the two. I felt so happy for them.

Pulling back clothes in Darcy's closet, I could clearly see there wasn't anything umm, well… fun. Let's just say it was all hang out clothing and not anniversary dinner clothing. Grabbing her hand and pulling her out of the closet she seemed to be thinking the same thing as me.

"Come on, you can look through my closet and see if there is anything in there you want to wear. I know sometimes I hate all my clothes and just want something new. It's been forever since someone borrowed anything from me. This will be fun."

On the way out I yelled back at Tim who was bringing his overnight bag back from the truck. "I'm going to makeover your wife tonight. Go dig through your closet. I know you have to at least have one pair of khakis and a nice shirt."

He smiled back at me and gave me a thumbs up. Darcy sat on my bed while I picked out possible outfits and held them up for her approval. It didn't seem like anything was going to work until I held up a black dress with sequins down the side. Her eyes lit up and I was surprised. This dress certainly didn't seem like anything she would ever want to wear.

"You know what, let's really surprise Tim and go with that one."

I did a fist pump into the air, "That's the spirit!"

We giggled like teenagers in the bathroom while we sipped on energy drinks mixed with vodka. I was just finishing the touches of winged eyeliner when the doorbell rang. It was Tim, he was wearing some khaki shorts and a gray button up. Hey, at least they aren't jeans. He had his hair brushed over in a charming, boyish combover.

When Darcy stepped out of the back hallway, his jaw literally dropped. It was quite a change to see her in a form fitting dress compared to her usual hospital scrubs. Her brown hair was resting over her shoulders, shining from the recent brushing. The dress clung to her curves in a way that even I was jealous of. She looked stunning. Her hands were held nervously in front of her, though, in a way that suggested she wasn't used to this kind of attention.

"Alright you kids have fun and don't do anything I wouldn't do." I teased them as I pushed them out the front door.

Tim was smiling ear to ear as he walked around to the passenger door and helped Darcy in. Walking around to the drivers side he waved happily before getting in and driving off.

Now what? The energy drink had me all jittery and I was feeling restless and lonely myself. I went inside and put on one of the discarded outfits from earlier. I put some mascara on and decided to go out and have some fun for myself too. Since moving here, I had only gone out with Darcy. She was keen on sticking together. I never went to any of the bars by myself.

I decided on Dave's Dive Bar because they had such a great atmosphere. It was also the place I was most familiar with. There was a band playing and the place was packed. I ordered myself a drink at the bar and was making my way through the crowd when a new song started to play. A man to my right flung up his hand in excitement and inadvertently hit my hand holding the cocktail. It went flying. Showering my legs as I tried to avoid most of the spill. Just as I was ready to let him have a piece of my mind, I looked up and was tethered to those bright blue eyes again. My mouth was hanging open... speechless.

I could tell he was about to apologize but then started smiling, "Well fancy running into you again. It's nice to see less of you." He was grinning now and it was contagious.

"Yes, you sure do have the moves. First you get a glimpse of the girls before we speak and now you've left me with something wet and sticky running down my leg. That usually doesn't happen until someone has taken me out on a proper date."

Now was the second time that night I saw a man's jaw drop. I couldn't hold my laughter in. Pretty soon, he was laughing too. We both held our stomachs and laughed until our cheeks hurt.

"Hello, I'm Elena. It's nice to finally get to introduce myself." I reach out my hand and he shakes it.

"I'm Noah. I just started at your agency as a temp for the next couple months."

Shifting to the side for some people making their way to the front, he motions for me to sit at the empty chair next to him and I do.

"Oh, I don't work at the nursing agency, I was actually dropping something off for my friend this morning. I usually don't go to work like a hot mess."

Those eyes again… I can feel my resolve to behave tonight slipping and full flirt mode is coming out.

"Well, it works for you. I just wish I had more papers to drop now." We both laugh again at this. "Let me at least buy you a drink to make up for the one you… umm… lost, down your legs."

"That would be great! I'll drink whatever you're having. I'm pretty easy." With that I blush, " I mean pretty easy going."

He smiles again and bites his lower lip. I am mesmerized. I wish I was doing that for him. Is it just me or did it get really hot in here all of a sudden? I pick up one of the menus on the table and start to fan myself as he turns and heads to the bar. *Get it together Elena! You are acting like such an idiot!* I think I have a handle on myself when he gets back to the table and sets my glass down. Our hands touch slightly and our touch sends shivers up my arm. I want more. He must sense it because he adjusts his chair to be closer to me.

"You come out here often?"

He tries to talk over the music but it's hard to hear. He sits closer and I can feel his breath on my neck as he is talking. Now it's like the heat that was in my face earlier has moved down, settling in my crotch and making it hard to think of anything else.

Swallowing before I drool down his neck, "Yeah, I actually come out with my friend, Darcy, she is the one who works with you."

"Oh, yeah. I met her this morning. She seems nice. Where is she tonight?"

Stirring my drink around and taking another sip before I reply, "She actually went out with her husband tonight for their anniversary."

He shakes his head at this, "And you? Any husband in your life?"

As he says this he looks down almost like he is waiting for the blow. "Umm… no, it's just me. And you?"

Now I'm the one biting my lip. He is looking up at me, directing those bold blue eyes my way, "It's just me."

The rest of the evening goes by in a blur. Drinks, music, laughing, me slapping his thigh at jokes and leaving it there to rest. I'm not sure how we ended up back at my place. I think it was me suggesting he check out my new hoya plant. He didn't believe me when I said they grew like hearts and he dared me to show him. If he said he wanted to see my plants, I couldn't deny him that, right?

Walking in the front door, I set my purse down on the couch and stuck my arms out wide in front of me to display my wooden shelves with my ever growing display of plants.

"This has been sort of my hobby lately. Taking these things and watching them grow. Nurturing them back to life. It's been like therapy."

He is trying to act interested, as he nods his head. I can sense him trying to ignore the energy in the room. Acting casually, I start to name off some of the plants and I find the hoya and point it out. When I look back, his eyes aren't on the plants at all. Almost like the pull of a magnet, I can feel something inside of me gravitating towards him. I'm not in control.

There is no denying this attraction and our bodies crash together with such force our teeth clink. It's like I was starving and he is the only thing that could nourish me. Our lips pressed together tightly and our bodies slammed against each other. His hand in my hair, wrapping it around his fist as he pulls my head back to kiss my neck. I groan out in pleasure and he walks me backward towards the wall. His lips are on mine again, as we lean against the wall. He is pushing against me. I can feel him straining against his pants as he leans down in front of me and slowly pulls my shorts down. He looks up at me. My eyes encourage him to continue. We find ourselves in my bedroom. How we ended up there, who knows. Our bodies seem to be made for each other as we both climax together.

He pulls me close to him and kisses my neck with such tenderness. I want to cry. I wrap my arms around him and return the favor. Rubbing his shoulders and back and leaving him kisses on his neck until our lips meet again.

My voice is raspy. "I promise, I could do this all night, but I need to get something to drink."

He reaches down to pull out and I see him make a confused face and knot his eyebrows together.

"What is it? What's wrong?" I ask concerned.

"Umm… I think the condom came off inside of you."

My eyes get big now, "Oh. Let me see if I can get it out."

After a couple awkward minutes, I was able to get the condom out. We are both staring at it as it lays on the comforter.

He is the first to talk, "So that's a first, are you on birth control?"

I haven't been on birth control in a long time, why would I? It's not like I've been in a serious relationship.

"No, but I'm close to my cycle, I doubt anything will happen."

With this he glances at me and smiles, "Oh things are going to happen."

And with this we make love again. I can feel something change. This time there is a softness to him, as if he already knows. That night, I fall asleep in his arms. It was the best night's sleep I've had in a long time. I've found home.

Darcy

The printer seems to be taking forever as it spits out a couple more papers. I still have 10 more to go and I start tapping my foot impatiently. This morning I'm already running behind schedule. Last night, Elena and I went out to a wing night at the restaurant down the road from her office. We ended up getting back home around 9:00 PM and stayed up late talking on the front porch.

We told stories about growing up. Her growing up in the hot Texas heat and me growing up in cold Ohio winters. This winter coming up would be the first time Elena has been around actual snow and icy roads. I joked with her about getting frostbite on her toes. She never wore sneakers – only sandals – even when it was raining. She had said she wanted to be completely free and only a blizzard would force her toes into boots. It was all fun and games until I went to bed after midnight. I slept right through my alarm clock this morning.

I was rushing and trying to get all my stuff together for the busy schedule I had today. I looked through my folder and noticed I didn't have some of the forms for my afternoon client. I had such a full schedule yesterday. I took some stuff home last night to finish up and figured I would get them signed today. I left them on the table this morning. In my race to get to the office this morning, I completely forgot them. I guess this is my fault after all. I knew Tim had a family gathering this weekend and I purposefully took on some extra appointments so I wouldn't have to go back home with him. I got to avoid being in a car with him for three hours and I avoided both our families. It was a win-win in my book.

Now I was being something I hated, unprepared. I would be very upset if I was late to my first appointment, as that could cause a snowball effect that would make me late to all the others too. I was never late for anything. I make it a priority to be at least five minutes ahead of time. Thinking ahead and being prepared was one of the reasons I had such a good reputation around here and why they let me have keys to the office. I had earned this spot.

I grabbed my phone and sent off a text to Elena hoping she had her phone near her. Thankfully she responds back quickly and agrees to bring my papers to me. Sighing a breath of relief, I can now wait on this stupid printer, get the rest of my stuff gathered for today's patients and make it on time.

I make a mental note to get her something as a thank you, maybe a new plant stand or something. Or we could go out to eat as she suggested. As I'm at the front desk organizing some forms, I hear the front door open. I look up to say thank you when I notice it's not Elena but a man in a gray shirt and athletic pants. He has dark, wavy hair, a cleft chin and most noticeably, striking blue eyes.

"Hey, I'm Noah. The new temp. I wasn't sure if you would be open today. I was just dropping off some papers I had to get finished from yesterday's meeting. I'm ready to get started."

He handed me the papers. He must think I am the receptionist. Next time, I'll make sure to have the door locked behind me when I swing by the office quick. I take the papers and leave them for Missy, the receptionist.

"I'm Darcy. One of the nurses here too. I'll leave this for them to get to on Monday so they can get you started. Thanks Goodbye."

I look down at my papers sending him clear signals that this conversation is over and I'm busy.

He takes the hint and turns to leave. "Thanks, see ya around."

Probably not pal. Not long after that Elena comes in the door. She looks frazzled as she hands me the papers and stands with her hands on her hips seemingly worked up about something. Her face is bright red.

"Umm… so the cutest guy just left and I bumped into him and he dropped some papers. When I leaned over to help him pick them up, I think I flashed him. I thought you said nobody was going to be here!"

We are walking to the door so I can lock up and leave. I can't believe she could be so careless. How could someone not stop and think about how they are presenting themselves? I would never leave the house without a bra on.

"You must have seen one of the new traveling nurses we just hired for a while. His name is Noah. We just met. I think he is here for like 13 weeks or something. Sometimes our office has traveling nurses pick up contracts temporarily when we are understaffed or we have someone leave for an extended period of time. One of our full-time people just went out on maternity leave. He is probably just covering for her. You won't have to worry about seeing him again."

I made sure the front door was locked up and we both headed to our cars. I'm thinking about my schedule for today and Noah is ancient history.

When I pull into the driveway, I'm ready to relax for the evening. I can see Elena sitting on the front porch. She sets her book down in her lap and looks in my direction. I walk over and sit beside her. I take a deep, relaxing breath, it really is a nice evening. The August heat seemed to finally lose its gusto. We can sit outside without feeling like we are melting away like a candle exposed to flame. Elena was just mentioning getting takeout when Tim's truck pulled into the driveway. I started to feel annoyed, especially when I saw him step out with flowers. He remembered, just when I thought we had made it through today.

"There's my beautiful wife! I know I wasn't supposed to come back until tomorrow; however, I was with my sister and she told me happy anniversary. I felt like a complete jerk. Please forgive me! I came back as soon as she reminded me. Let me take you out tonight!"

Both he and Elena were smiling at me and I know I would look like a total jerk if I didn't agree to this. Here I am acting like this is a great idea. I stand to take the flowers from Tim and he kisses me right on the cheek. Great, now I know how my night is going to end. Flowers and dinner mean he is probably going to be expecting something else later. This is my anniversary too. If I got what I wanted, he would be back at his parents and I would be crawling into bed alone. I guess this is something I need to do to keep everything the way it's supposed to be. Keep everyone else happy. Elena came in to help me get ready. Not that I needed to be reminded that I had the most boring closet. She was moving hospital scrubs and plain shirts around in my closet looking for what she called, "something fun". Although this wasn't the closet of someone fun, this was the closet of a planner. Someone who worked hard and didn't let herself fall into any situations that could leave her hurt again. Elena's eyes brightened and I already knew what she was going to suggest before she said it.

"Come on, you can look through my closet and see if there is anything in there you want to wear. I know sometimes I hate all my clothes and just want something new. It's been forever since someone borrowed anything from me. This will be fun."

I sat on her bed while she held up different options for me, they were all too much. Too much color, too many ruffles… just so not me. Then she pulled up the black dress, the one with the sequins that danced in the light and I wanted that one. I was surprised by my choice and I knew Elena was surprised when I saw Elena raise her eyebrows. Why not, right?

We mixed up some drinks and while I got ready in her bathroom we laughed about what possible outfit Tim was going to come up with. I speculated that he might have to get a forklift to go through his shirt collection and find something that could pass for a nice dinner outfit. Elena was helping me with my makeup when we heard Tim at the door. The effects of the vodka were kicking in and I was feeling giddy. Like I was getting ready for the prom that I had skipped out on before.

Elena went to the door and I was there, all alone in front of the mirror, as I looked at the woman staring back at me. See I thought to myself, you made it work, now things are on the way up. Everything is going to get better. I turned the light off and walked out. Little did I know, if I would have stayed in the bathroom a little longer, I would have seen my reflection shaking her finger at me and saying see I told you this would end up just like before. But I was already gone, too impatient to let any practical thoughts form and warn me about where this was heading.

I can't remember the last time I wore something form fitting like this. I felt a little exposed standing there. The dress clinging to me so tightly. I kept trying to pull it up a little to cover my cleavage. Tim's mouth dropped open and then I felt annoyed. He is going to be all over me later. Looks like I'll be getting wasted tonight.

We ended up going to an Italian restaurant and eating in their wine cellar. It was a candlelit dinner and very romantic. By the time we were ready to leave, I was feeling a little tipsy and Tim had to help me to the car. I was feeling good. While we were driving I tried to apply some of the lipstick that Elena had lent me. Tim went over a bump and it went up my cheek. We both started laughing. It felt good to be happy. I was feeling glad I went.

When we pulled into the driveway, I noticed Elena's car was gone. Hmm, I sent her a quick text to see where she was.

> Hey, we just got back. Where did you head off to?

Tim looks over at me and says, "Hey, don't worry. I'm sure she will be back soon. Let's worry about us."

Yeah, right, he was probably just worried about his boner. I just hoped she was going to get back soon. About an hour later, we had changed into our usual Saturday night lounge clothes. I was enjoying another drink when Tim offered to rub my shoulders.

At the same time I heard my phone ping, "Sure, hold on one second I think that's Elena."

OMG! I'm talking to that guy Noah from earlier. HE IS SO CUTE! I'm at Dave's Bar and we are watching the live band. Having lots of fun. I'm safe and will be home soon. Hope your dinner went great! Talk later xoxo

Well, at least I know who she is with. I let Tim guide me into the bedroom for *my anniversary massage*. Come on, like he really just wants to only rub my shoulders. Whatever... let's get this out of the way. I turn the lights off and let him massage my back. I know what comes next. He uses this ruse everytime he is interested in having sex. It's not that I mind though. It gives me a clear view into what is coming. It seems to work for us because if I say yes, he knows he will get lucky. If I decline he resorts to his gaming system for the night. He says the best massage is a naked massage so I take off my clothes for him. This next part doesn't take long because he starts with a massage. Soon he directs me to lay on my side while he slides next to my body and guides himself into me. Then I close my eyes and take a deep breath thinking of my schedule for the next day and waiting for him to finish.

I climb out of bed and go to the bathroom to clean myself. When I come back out, he is already asleep. In the room next to ours I can hear faint sounds, I walk over and put my ear against the wall. Sure enough, I can hear Elena in there with someone. Probably that guy, Noah. So gross. She barely knows him. That's one of the things I just don't get about her – the spontaneity and being so free all the time. If she doesn't watch it, her trust and free love is going to get her in over her head with the wrong person. She is lucky she has me to watch over her and make sure she is safe.

THE FIRST TRIMESTER

Elena

Monday seems to drag on. I keep checking my phone to see if there is a new text from Noah. We could barely tear ourselves away from each other this morning. We needed to get back to our jobs. The clinic was counting on me and Noah needed to start his onboarding for his contract at the nursing agency.

After our long, steamy night Saturday we finally roused ourselves out of bed around noon and cleaned up (together, of course). I suggested we go out for Sunday brunch. By the time I grabbed my phone out of my purse, I had nine text messages from Darcy. She was mostly just checking in on me to see what I wanted to do for the day.

Noah leaned over my shoulder to nibble my wet hair and saw my screen. "She must really miss you. Tell her she can have you every other Wednesday and weekend. Well, maybe just the wednesdays."

Laughing he pulled me in close for another kiss and I felt the heat again. "Hey now, we really need to take a break. I'm starving. I need to recharge if I'm going to survive your stamina."

Smiling, I grabbed his hand and my purse and headed out the door. We spent the rest of the day together and even went to see a movie. Both of us prolonging when we would have to leave each other. He suggested seeing that hoya plant again, and just like that we started all over.

Now that I was away from him, I was constantly checking my watch. Seven more hours of my shift… I felt like this might be one of the slowest days of my life. I about jumped when my phone pinged,

Hey Gorgeous! Today is going soo slow...I'm almost done with my orientation and I'm getting ready to head out to my first patient of the day. Probably will be too busy to talk much. I'm sure I'll be thinking about you all day long...I'll call when I'm done.

    Holding my phone in both hands, I bring it to my chest as if in prayer. I can't stop smiling. I've never felt this way before and certainly have never been left feeling this way physically. I'm sore in all the right places. It's only been a couple days since we met but I just feel so comfortable around him. My most serious relationship, which lasted almost a year, wasn't as intense as the past 24 hours. I know some of the clients that come in for therapy come as a requirement for drug rehab. I'm tempted to ask them if this is what it feels like to be addicted to something. That first time being such a high that nothing else in the world seems to matter. You feel invincible. When you are left without that rush, you want it back in the worst way. It seems like Noah is always on my mind. I'm counting down the seconds until we see each other again.

    Another text and it takes barely a second to see it since my phone is still in my hands. I'm willing Noah to text me, hoping he is feeling the same way. It's a text from Darcy though. Shoot! I've yet to text her back.

I'm sorry for another text but I was just getting worried. Are you mad at me or something? Can you please just let me know what's going on?

    I feel bad about not getting back to Darcy and responding sooner. I quickly sent her a text to explain the reason why it took me so long to reply, hoping she will accept my apology.

I'm so SORRY! I just got carried away hanging out with Noah this weekend. We are really hitting it off and having so much fun! Didn't mean to leave you hanging like that. I'm hoping he can do dinner later after work but I can stop over and see you when we get back. Or maybe we can all go out to eat later this week if Tim is off. I'm okay and don't worry k xoxo

To keep me on task, I begrudgingly put my phone in my purse, under my feet, at my desk. I pulled out my to-do list and tried for one of my most productive days. I want to pass the time and keep my mind out of the gutter.

It seems we find a new rhythm to the week. We both get off work and meet up at my place. Then, we head out for dinner and I show him some of the places I'm familiar with. Then, we check out something new together. Then, we head back to my place and make love until we fall asleep in each other's arms. Then, we wake up, make love again and start all over.

I didn't see much of Darcy that week. It seems like she is working late or avoiding me. I haven't seen her come out of the house, when her car is home. Maybe she knows I truly need this. She might have known how lonely I was.

By the time Friday rolls around, Noah is grabbing some clothes out of his suitcase. I'm curious about where he is supposed to be staying. I'm feeling a little worried he might be getting sick of me.

"So when you do these traveling contracts, where do you stay? I mean if you want to get unpacked I can check with Darcy about her weekend plans. I just feel bad you haven't had the chance to really get situated or anything."

I'm twirling my hair, on the bed, when he lays down next to me, enveloping me in his strong arms. If I was a cat, I'd purr right now.

"I usually stay in a little studio apartment. I once stayed in a tiny bedroom above someone's garage. This time, I'm staying in a cute little duplex surrounded by plants and one of the most beautiful women I've ever seen. That is, if she wants me around."

While he is talking, I can't see his face and I think he made it this way on purpose. I have my head resting on his chest. While I'm rubbing his chest, I quickly move my hand up to wipe a tear away. I'm overjoyed.

"Umm… so I get to have my own personal sex slave, on demand, for the next couple months. Hmm… let me think about that one."

At this, he laughs and pulls me closer to him. I hear him exhale and realize he was holding his breath.

"But seriously, it's no big deal. I was booked in a motel room until I found something else that worked for the meantime. My agency just gives me a stipend to pay for housing. I'd be glad to help you with rent while I'm here. Or, maybe, I'll just keep the money as pay since I'll be your on call sex slave."

He laughs at this. I can't get over how easy it is with him and wonder if there is truly love at first sight. Would I be lucky enough to have that happen to me? I remember my grandmother telling me she was only with her husband for four months before they were married. I felt so incredulous, while listening to her story. But here I am, with Noah, living together after one week. Her story doesn't seem so far-fetched anymore.

That morning, after we decided on living arrangements, we sealed the deal with a kiss. I found myself reluctantly at work. I'm getting ready to look over my emails when I decide to send a quick text to Darcy to check in and let her know my crazy news.

> Soo….Noah is going to stay with me until his contract is up! I know that sounds crazy and you are probably rolling your eyes, but he is such a great guy! I would love for all of us to get together this weekend and hang out. Hope everything is going great with you guys too! XOXO

For some reason, I sense she is going to be mad after I hit send. Her surprisingly upbeat response about meeting up and getting to know Noah has me feeling relieved. That's one of the bad things with communicating through text, you never get to see the person. Words can often be misunderstood. Facial expressions that can be seen while talking face-to-face are hidden by yellow smiley-face emojis. Providing a false pretense, to the true thoughts, or feelings from their sender.

Darcy

Holding the glass up to the light, I inspect it for any bits of dust I might have left. Satisfied, I put it back on the shelf and grab the next one. I've been cleaning and dusting all morning. Feeling uneasy about the fact that Elena still hasn't texted back or left the house. My restless energy is now being used to make sure the house is spotless; something I do when I'm feeling anxious. I'm bored too. Elena and I have been spending our downtime together and it feels strange to think of a time when she wasn't living here. Even though it's been a short period of time, I've come to rely on her for keeping me entertained. Left on my own, I don't want to go back to binge watching sitcoms or reading on my days off. Tim is still sleeping from his late shift delivering last night and probably won't get up for a couple more hours. When he wakes up, he will most likely just eat a bowl of cereal in front of the tv and not be of any help at all.

Putting the glass down, I grab my phone and send another text. At this point I should probably stop. That was my ninth text since last night. I'm getting worried and a little annoyed. Yeah, she let me know who she was with, but I can't believe she let him stay the night! Now it's like she forgot about me or something.

Sliding the phone back into my pocket so I dont miss her text, I get back to dusting. Around noon, Tim comes into the living room with his bowl. He had to step over the vacuum cord, as I have the nozzle attachment out, and am going around the baseboard trying to get anything I might have missed from earlier.

I hear Elenas front door open. I'm on my knees but I straighten up trying to gauge whether she is walking towards my door or not. Tim seems to pause too, spoon in his mouth and eyebrows raised. He is trying to listen to what I'm straining to hear. He gives up and continues eating. Chomp, chomp, chomping away, milk dribbling down his chin.

Looking back, I hear her car start up and I walk over to the curtain; pulling it back slightly to look out. The car is backing out and they are both inside, smiling and talking animatedly. I pull my phone out of my back pocket to check the battery. It isn't dead. Full charge and zero notifications.

My house is the cleanest it's ever been. I even got Tim to put on clean clothes. I've wiped down his game consoles. She still isn't home. Tim seems to be getting concerned with my cleaning. He gently comes over and puts the glasses back on the shelf when I take one down to start again.

"Hey, look it's okay. I know today was a change in your schedule and you miss her, but it's okay. Look, let's go put a movie on in the bedroom and relax and I'll give you a foot rub." At this, he holds his hands up as if to show me he has no intentions for anything else. "You have worked hard today and the house looks great."

I admit defeat and put the glass back up on the shelf and let him lead me to the bedroom. We end up putting on some romantic comedy. Tim is cracking up. I feign drowsiness and roll over closing my eyes. Tim takes the hint and turns the movie and lights off and resigns for the evening to his game system. Checking my phone one last time, I see nothing. I get up quietly and sneak my reserve bottle of vodka out of the bottom of my night stand and drink while reading up on the news on my phone until the lines blur together and my head starts to get heavy.

Swallowing down two extra strength ibuprofen and slipping my sunglasses on the next day, I'm hoping this hangover doesn't last that long. Lately, I haven't been drinking that much. Last night I overdid it. This Monday is going to be so long. Exhaling as I sit in the driveway, getting ready to see my first client. I look at my phone laying on the front seat and decide to send a text to Elena. I know she came home last night because her car was in the driveway, when I left for work. It's not like she crashed or something. I know that I can appeal to her if I send this text making her think she has left me hurting. I make it sound like I'm upset at something she did to make me sad; knowing full well that she immediately will want to fix things.

> I'm sorry for another text but I was just getting worried. Are you mad at me or something? Can you please just let me know what's going on?

Instantly I get a reply back, just as I anticipated.

I'm so SORRY! I just got carried away hanging out with Noah this weekend. We are really hitting it off and having so much fun! Didn't mean to leave you hanging like that. I'm hoping he can do dinner later after work but I can stop over and see you when we get back. Or maybe we can all go out to eat later this week if Tim is off. I'm okay and don't worry
k xoxo

So again with Noah. I'm glad he is only a temp and will be gone soon. Hopefully they both tire of each other soon and this fizzles out. I don't understand the need for some people to always be all over each other. The amount of sex in the media and on television disgusts me. I check in with the office and let them know I can take extra appointments this week. I ask that they put me on call to cover for anybody else. If she is going to be busy this week, then so am I. How about she get a taste of her own medicine and see what it feels like to be left alone and bored. Satisfied with myself, I put my phone on silent and get started with my day.

The week is busy and when I'm not working, I run errands. I strategically arrange my time so that I avoid her comings and goings. When I'm at home, I make it a point to keep the shades drawn and lights off to avoid seeing her. I sit in the back of the house, at the kitchen table, sipping wine and playing word games, on my phone. Friday, I switch some appointments around so I can be working in the evening instead of the morning.

I'm sitting cross-legged, on the bed, watching a morning talk show when my phone pings next to me. It's from Elena. As I read the text my disbelief quickly turns into anger. I can't believe she is letting Noah move in with her. She must be crazy. She hardly knows him! For a minute, I'm tempted to just move on with my life and forget about her. It's too much drama. It's not like I need her. I was doing fine before. Then a plan starts to come into focus. I can hang out with her regularly. Tim and I can go on dates together with them. We can reduce the amount of time they have together. She won't have as much time to invest in Noah and he will get restless and start to look around for something else. With a renewed interest, I sat up straight in bed and hurriedly texted her back.

> Wow, that is fast but only you right!? Ha! I'm happy for you and actually think that it would be nice for Tim and I to hang out with you guys and get to know Noah! I've been busy this week with work. How about we all get together tomorrow night! I'm texting Tim right now to get someone to cover his shift. See ya at 6pm for beer and wings. Let's all drive together. This will be so much fun! ☺

Laying back in bed feeling relaxed, I intertwine my fingers and put them behind my head. I'm already planning more dates together for next week. I know she won't deny time with me when she sees how excited I am for them. She won't be able to say no to me. That's the problem with people like her. They are too nice and that's what gets them into trouble. She needs me to make sure this Noah guy can be trusted and is good enough. If not, in the end, he will end up hurting her… or worse.

Elena

Rummaging through my jewelry box, I found the other stud I was looking for. As I'm putting it in, I turn and see that Noah is on his hands and knees reaching under my bed. His hand is pulling out a box. The earring drops from my hand, as I rush over to push it back under. Surprised, he sits back as if it were him I had pushed.

"Geez. I was just trying to get my other shoe. I was going to look around that box. I'm not snooping. Now I'm curious about what you had in there. Was it sex toys? Am I right? I mean what girl keeps a box labeled special stuff under her bed."

Leaning down, I reach under the bed until my fingers reach the sneaker and I pull it out, giving it to him. I'm smiling, but inside I'm rattled. That was close.

"No. It's not sex toys. Pervert. It's just important documents. You know, like my birth certificate and stuff like that."

As I look for my dropped earring, I can see him out of the corner of my eye.

"I see, well maybe we should get you a proper, special sex box in the future."

Picking up the stud I put it in. Motioning for him to come out with me.

"Well let's go get some beer and wings."

Placing a kiss on my head, he grabs my hand and we head next door, to meet Tim and Darcy, for our dinner plans. As we are leaving, I remind myself that I will need to hide the box in my closet when we get back. Probably under some old blankets, where it would be safer. I can't imagine him opening up the box and seeing what was really in there. The past I ran away from but can't bear to throw away. Who could love someone who did what I did?

The bar is smoky and packed with customers. The hostess tells us the wait time for food is over an hour. Tim suggests a game of pool while we wait for our food. Pretty soon, the guys are engaged in a competition. Winner buys beer for the night.

I'm glad for the chance to hang out and for Noah to meet my friends. It looks like Tim feels the same way as he kids around with Noah and teases him about all the beer he will be drinking later. He hopes Noah is ready to do some overtime for the bill. I'm not surprised though. Tim is so easy going. Noah jokes around that he can't get too wasted or I'll take advantage of him later when we get home. While he is chalking the end of his pool stick, he looks over and winks at me. Smiling, I turn back to Darcy. She is sitting on one of the two stools we nabbed by the pool tables. She has been drinking pretty steadily since we got here. I can tell she is buzzed as she smiles and does a hoot for Tim.

"Come on Tim, whoop him good and add my drinks to his tab."

My feelings are mixed about how I'm feeling. Her sudden interest in going out and being so chatty with me and Tim is very confusing. Of course, I'm glad to see her coming out of her shell. At the same time, it feels off. Like she is forcing this side of her. I can't understand what she would be getting out of this.

When our food is ready and we are seated, Tim holds his beer up as if it were a trophy.

He triumphantly says, "To my worthy opponent, he thought he got the best of me, but he was no match for the prolific skills of Tim the pool master."

At this we all raise our drinks and toast to the winner.

"Now, as a nurse, I care about everyone's health and suggest we switch to water to prevent dehydration on this warm night."

Noah puts on a serious face but then breaks into a big smile when Tim matches his serious face too. They both burst out laughing. Darcy, who has been quiet for the past several minutes, raises her glass and says she would like to make an announcement. We quiet down and listen.

"So, I actually wanted to surprise you all with something. I know that we all have been working pretty hard and decided we should reward ourselves with some well-deserved time off. That is why I booked a cabin near Hocking Hills State Park, for next weekend. We all can enjoy Labor Day weekend together!"

I'm not sure who is more surprised, me or Tim. Ready for any adventure, Tim lifts his glass up again and gives out a whoop.

"Hope they have pool tables there, too."

This time, it's Darcy with the triumphant smile as she raises her glass and clinks it with mine. I can't help but wonder what her prize is. Instead, I shrug off my apprehension and ask myself *Isn't this what I wanted, to make Darcy feel more comfortable and that I was her friend?* I can't help but sense something else. I can't quite put my finger on it. Maybe that's the problem with what happened before, I'll always be paranoid. Constantly looking for something wrong in people when there isn't anything to find.

Packing my suitcase into the car, I shut the trunk and feel my spirits lift. I see Noah pulling into the spot next to me. He is dressed in gray scrubs and holds up five fingers to me as he sprints to the door.

"Give me five minutes to clean up and grab my bag."

I nod at him as I lean back against the warm car, closing my eyes to the sun and letting it warm my body. I'm glad that we could get off early and head to the park before Tim and Darcy. It seems this week every time Noah and I wanted to head out or were just going to sit down to eat Darcy would get home and ask to tag along or stop over to say hi. Not that we cared. I did want to have a couple hours alone with Noah to hang out and connect after the week.

I went through the contents of my suitcase in my head, feeling again like I had forgotten something. Hmm… Oh well. If I need something once we get there, we can just run to the store.

Noah comes running out of the house. His hair is wet and he has a bag slung over his shoulder. Mmm… the way his arm muscles bulge as he holds his bag makes my stomach do a little flip. I rethink my idea of talking when we get there. Maybe there is something else we can do to pass the time. He locks up the door and walks over to give me a kiss.

"Alright, let's get this show on the road."

Typing in the address on the GPS I grin at him in the front seat, "Looking forward to this weekend with you, babe." Reaching over he takes my hand and squeezes it. Just like that we hold hands the whole way to the park.

It turns out to be a beautiful place. We have a rustic log cabin with a big back deck and a built-in hot tub overlooking the woods. We spend the weekend hiking, kayaking and trying out new recipes on the grill.

Noah and Tim decide to go on a beer run, on Sunday evening, while Darcy and I relax in the hot tub. It is our last night here. We put on some soft rock and slip into some bikinis. The hot tub's temperature is perfect. I pile my hair into a big messy bun and sit back and relax. The jets work into my muscles and I find myself closing my eyes and zoning out. Suddenly, it hits me. My eyes fly open and I sit up straight.

Darcy jerks back, confused by my reaction, "What's wrong with you?"

My brain is racing in all different directions. I remembered what I should have brought with me on this trip. What I should have needed earlier this week too.

My voice seems small as I quietly respond, "I didn't get my period this week."

At this, Darcy goes still, too. Her face was serious. I wonder what she is thinking when she doesn't say anything and gets out of the hot tub. She wraps a towel around her as she sits on a wooden adirondack chair and turns the music off on her phone. My anxiety is starting to build and I'm still in a daze thinking about what the chances are that it just might be late when she looks up at me from her phone.

Her voice seems to be lost as she says something so quiet I have to ask her to repeat herself. Instead of saying anything, she holds her phone up for me to see. I'm looking at a big – 6 and in tiny words underneath it says *days until expected period.*

This time she seems to find her voice, "I'm six days late. I'm never late."

Leaning back in the hot tub I find that while I'm surprised, I'm also feeling a little bit of happiness spread through my body. My eyes start to water.

"Darcy, I can't believe this! Do you think we could actually be, you know, at the same time?!"

Darcy puts down her phone and seems to be thinking about this, "It would have to be the night of our anniversary. I'm on birth control and I just don't understand how this happened."

Moving my hands under the water I feel my tummy to see if maybe there is a bump there I might not have noticed.

"Oh, I know how this happened. Tim put his good ol 'dance moves on for you and you couldn't resist it. Oh my, Tim and Noah will be back any minute! What do we tell them? There is no way I can keep this secret. They went to get us wine coolers."

Standing up, Darcy slips off her bottoms and pulls up her shorts. She slips on her sandals and looks at my confused expression.

"Well, come on. Let's go! We need to get some pregnancy tests and check this out."

I sent a text to Noah and Tim letting them know we had to run out really quick and would be right back. Darcy doesn't talk the whole trip to the pharmacy. When we returned to the cabin, the guys still weren't there. We each hurry to a bathroom and meet back up in the kitchen.

"Let's go to the back porch. We might as well sit down while we wait." I suggest.

Putting the tests on the balcony, I set a timer on my phone and try to patiently wait the recommended 2 minutes. Darcy paces back and forth in front of me. One hand to her mouth and the other rubbing her shoulder. The timer on my phone chirps at us and she stops. She is staring at the stick.

"You check it, I can't bear to look."

First, I go to the one I put there, on the right. Then, I look at hers. Darcy is staring at me.

"Well, what do they say?"

Now my hands are covering my mouth as I break out in a huge smile. I pull her close for a hug and squeeze her as the words, "We are pregnant," come out!

At that exact moment, Noah and Tim walk through the doorway. Both are holding brown paper bags. They stop with frozen, shocked expressions.

Tim is the first to say something but it's more like a jumble, "You're-pregnant-I-can't-believe-this-I'm-so-happy?!"

The longest, happiest word he has probably ever said. He reaches for Darcy and pulls her out of my embrace and picks her right up, twirling her on the porch. She is still in the same position, obviously shocked as he puts her down.

I look up at Noah who is still standing in the doorway. I'm wondering what is going through his mind. I don't have to wait long. He sets the bag down and as he steps closer. I see his eyes are watering and a tear escapes as he pulls me close to him and kisses my head. Burying his face in my hair, we hold tight to one another.

He leans to my ear and whispers, "I am so happy, I love you."

Now I'm the one crying. Soon, Tim comes over and hugs us too. I reach out and pull a still shocked Darcy into the embrace. We all stand there, hugging. I close my eyes and take this moment in. The warmth of our bodies, the smell of the forest and the slight chlorine smell of the hot-tub. The sound of the crickets chirping, the feeling of hope, happiness and a chance to have a family rushing over me.

Through it all, I try to push back the thoughts that I don't deserve this. Not after what I did. As this baby grows inside of me and we are one, I hope it doesn't have access to my thoughts and memories. Because then it would be swimming in a sea of tears instead of amniotic fluid.

Darcy

Jumping up from the couch, Tim scurries to answer the door. Ever since I told him to cancel work because we were going out, he has been acting like an excited puppy. I'm surprised he doesn't jump up on them when they come through the door. I'll admit, it's tough being with someone so sociable. I like to think it's one of the reasons it works for us. He does all the talking and is so animated that everyone pays attention to him. I'm more of an afterthought. His friends all refer to me as "Tim's wife". Noah and Elena walk into the room hand-in-hand.

They look more comfortable than I expected. There is an energy between them I can't quite put my finger on. Almost like they feed into each other. I'm not surprised, being around her is like being hooked up to an IV vitamin therapy. I've heard of patients who have used it and said it gives them renewed energy and boosts them mentally. Elena used to give that to me. I want it back. She comes over to me and I stand to get going but she wraps her arms around me and gives me a hug.

"I've missed you Darcy! Thanks for inviting us tonight."

As she pulls away, my insecurity about this social outing lightens. I feel I could almost do this without alcohol. Almost.

We have to drive down the street to find parking. It's busy tonight. The hostess at the bar tells us the wait for a table and food is about an hour. Tim points in the direction of the pool tables.

"Anybody up for a game? Maybe we could make it so the winner pays for the beer tonight?"

Noah grins, "Oh, my man, you're on! Just don't start crying when you lose."

I roll my eyes as Elena links arms with me and declines playing, "You knuckleheads go ahead. I'm going to catch up with Darcy. Come on, let's get some drinks and grab a table."

I settle on rum and soda, asking for doubles. It doesn't take me long to loosen up and start to relax. I'm really getting into this game and hanging out. I even find myself cheering Tim on. Encouraged by my interest in him, he puffs his chest out and starts playing with more confidence. Maybe I should actually pay attention to him more.

Looking over, I catch Elena looking at me curiously. I just smile back and feel content that I have her right where I want her. Thinking she is mending her broken plant of a friend. HA! Our attention is caught by Tims loud whooping as he starts doing his patented celebratory victory dance. The one I've often seen from his gaming conquests at home. Noah just shakes his head. I see him look over our way and shrug his shoulders.

"Guess I'm paying for your drinks tonight, hope you guys are lightweights."

Our pager goes off and we all go find a hostess to be seated. After some more gloating from Tim, I couldn't contain my excitement anymore and decided to let everyone know my plan for the upcoming Labor Day weekend.

Raising my glass, "So, I actually wanted to surprise you all with something. I know that we all have been working pretty hard and decided we should reward ourselves with some well-deserved time off. That is why I booked a cabin near Hocking Hills State Park, for next weekend. We all can enjoy Labor Day weekend together!"

Tim and Darcy both widen their eyes and I know they must be surprised. Not just at our getaway, but that I was the one to suggest and plan it for everyone. What they don't know is how much trouble I actually went through to make this all work on short notice. Everything was booked and I ended up paying an extra $500 bucks just so the one guy on the booking site would cancel the other guests and let me take over the cabin.

Tim, with his never ending enthusiasm, gets excited all over again. I knew he would be. He loves anything new and adventurous. I'm pleased with myself for thinking this all through. I know by the end of next weekend Elena and Noah will be ready to take some time apart. If I know one thing for sure, Elena is the loyal kind. I'll be around so much Noah will be sure to say something wrong and she will kick him to the curb. See ya later, Noah.

During the week, I make excuses to stop over and see them in the evening. Choosing to stay until late. If Elena and Noah want to go out to dinner, I'll invite myself along. They both act very happy and seem to love having me around. I know this is probably driving Noah crazy though. My last client of the day runs over schedule on Friday, so I text Elena to go ahead without us. Tim and I will catch up later. After I get home, Tim is waiting by the door with his small overnight bag packed, stepping over it to get to the bedroom. I wonder how the guy even manages anything on his own. He probably forgot underwear and a toothbrush. Grabbing my already packed bag, I change out of my scrubs and freshen up in the bathroom. Pulling my hair back into a ponytail, I smile at myself in the mirror before turning the lights off. *This weekend is going to go just as planned.*

My only goal of the weekend is to get a closer look at Noah and Elena's relationship. I want to know just how serious they are. I actually find myself having a good time. Maybe it's all the fresh air and sunshine. We went on a hike, checked out the natural waterfalls, rented kayaks and hung out on the lake. I've not allowed myself to have fun for so long that it almost feels like I'm breaking the rules somehow. I feel myself start to break free from my past confinements. Maybe it's time to move on.

Noah and Elena seem to be head over heels for each other. They are constantly stealing glances at one another and when they are close to each other there is always some form of physical contact. I found it rubbing off on Tim and I, too. I tolerated Tim placing his arm on my shoulder and letting it rest there as we watched a movie, in the den.

By the end of the day, on Sunday, Tim suggests getting some beer for him and Noah. I asked if he could pick us up some wine coolers for the hot tub.

Looking at Elena, I said, "Let's get a head start and get in now."

She was sitting on the stool in the living room, but jumped up excitedly!

"Yes, I'll go get my swimsuit on!"

We meet up on the back porch. This is one of my favorite parts of the cabin. A large wooden deck overlooking the forest, with a built-in hot tub to the side. I wish I could live here everyday. I select a station on my phone to play 70's rock and step into the hot tub slowly. I sit back and feel the jets working my worries away. Suddenly, Elena sits up straight and startles me.

"What's wrong with you?"

She has this bewildered look on her face. I'm just about to turn my head to see if there is some creature coming out of the woods behind me, when she finally finds her voice.

"I didn't get my period this week."

As I hear the words, a feeling of dread comes over me and my own realization sets in. During my busy week working and tagging along with her and Noah, I hadn't noticed my own missed period. *This can't be right!* Getting out of the hot tub, I wrap my towel around my dripping body and grab my phone with shaking hands. I find the app I was looking for. Hesitating for just a second, I touch it and immediately the number 6 appears before my eyes. I'm used to seeing it with a (+) before it indicating how many days until my cycle will start again. No this has (-) before it, indicating how late I am.

"I can't believe this."

Elena leans forward in the hot tub, "Darcy, I couldn't understand you, what is it?"

Now I'm the one finding my voice again, as I take a swallow to coat my dry throat.

"I'm six days late. I'm never late."

"Darcy, I can't believe this! Do you think we could actually be, you know, at the same time?!"

She leans back in the hot tub almost seeming to soak this up with happiness like the sun we were enjoying earlier. I see her hand go to her stomach, under the water. As she feels it, a small smile starts to play on her lips. I have the opposite reaction as I reach for my stomach. I actually think I might throw up. I'm not sure if we are really "you know", as Elena suggested, but I have to find out right now! I look around on the deck for the shorts I had slipped off earlier and start changing right there. Elena looks over confused by what I'm doing.

"Well, come on. Let's go. We need to get some pregnancy tests and check this out."

As we walk out to the car, Elena sends a quick text to the guys to let them know we went to the store and would be right back. On the drive to the pharmacy, I can't think about anything else. I'm willing my brain to focus on the tasks ahead. One step at a time. Turn right… put your foot on the gas pedal… left turn signal… turn left… walk into the pharmacy… This is something I've done before. I have a feeling of deja vu as I walk up to the cashier and hand her 2 tests. I feel the judgment in her eyes on me. She knows what I've done. Grabbing them quickly, and not waiting for change or a receipt, I walk back out to the car. Elena stares out the window on the drive; lost in her own thoughts too.

When we get back, I make a beeline for the bathroom in the back bedroom. I take the little stick out, peeing on the end. I go back out to the kitchen and meet up with Elena. She is holding her identical stick. She suggests we go out to the back porch and wait together. She sits down and sets the timer on her phone. I can't sit down. All this nervous energy is coursing through my body.

I already know that the test will say I'm pregnant. I try to enjoy the last two minutes of still living in the unknown. A world where I'm not pregnant. Tomorrow, I'll go back home and everything will be the same. I know one thing, if by some small chance I'm not pregnant, I'm going to beg my doctor to give me a hysterectomy.

The timer pings to us from the armrest of the chair like the sound of guns firing from an execution squad, killing any hope I have. Elena seems to move in slow motion as she checks her test then mine. I can't tell the meaning of her beaming smile until she grabs me close, saying the words aloud.

"We are pregnant!"

Rounding the corner of the back door at the same time, I see Noah and Tim standing there. *Oh Crap!* Tim runs to me and while I'm still reeling from the news he picks me up and spins me on the spot. Pulling me close, I can feel his heart pounding through his shirt. This is all happening too fast. I need to sit and take this all in. This time there is no hiding it.

Glancing over at Noah, I check to see his reaction. I can see his eyes water as he rushes to Elena and they embrace. Their faces close so I can't quite tell what they are saying. When they pull back, I can see tears on both of their faces.

Tim rushes over to hug and congratulate them. Elena reaches out, catching my arm, and pulls me in for a group hug. I close my eyes and try to relax my body. My shoulders feel as if they are about to touch my ears. The only thing I hear is the blood pounding in my head. I wonder if people who have killed their first child could ever really be fit to be mothers. As this baby grows and opens its eyes, will it see the tiny scratch marks on the walls of my uterus where its previous sibling tried to hold on before it was ripped out of me to meet its untimely death.

Elena

If I had ever imagined things could get any better with Noah, this would be it. He is attentive to all my needs. I feel like I'm walking on clouds. The only thing tethering me to the ground is the time when I'm not with him. We are laying together on my bed watching a movie while he is rubbing my feet. It's been almost a month since we came back from our labor day getaway. During that time, I had gone in for an appointment, at the walk-in clinic, to get my pregnancy confirmed.

My first OBGYN appointment is scheduled in October and we are looking forward to the first checkup. He has bought all kinds of pregnancy books. They sit on the coffee table with the prenatal vitamins he bought. I find it amazing that he is so involved.

Sitting up in bed, I reach for my water and take small sips. This morning the nausea kicked in. I was coming out of the bathroom, towel in hand, drying my hair. Noah had just finished frying some sausages. I'm not sure what brand he was using today, but the smell was so intense. It seemed to go right down my nose and explode into my stomach. I reached the kitchen wastebasket just in time to throw up. I haven't stopped since. I called off of work. I spent the day munching on crackers and sipping water. Regularly running to the toilet and throwing up until there was nothing left. My body wouldn't be satisfied until it saw the green bile of my stomach.

Thankfully, today was Friday. Noah looks over at me with his concerned face again.

"Do you want me to get you some ginger ale?"

Thinking back to earlier when I had some to calm my stomach, I make a face.

"Ugh. No! I tried that earlier and ended up throwing up and it fizzled all the way up my nose. I don't think I'll try that again for a long time."

He slides up so he is sitting next to me and starts looking up morning sickness remedies on his phone.

"Well, ginger is supposed to be really good for nausea. How about I order some of these candies and gum? They have excellent ratings."

Shrugging my shoulders, "Sure, I'll try anything to start feeling better."

While he is tapping away, on his phone, I gather up my courage to ask him the question I've been thinking about the most today.

"So, I know you mentioned your parents live in Nebraska, have you told them yet?"

Looking down at my hands, as they rest on my stomach, I bring my eyes back up to look at him. Locking onto those blue eyes for the question I want to ask, but fear the most.

"What does this mean for us?"

His face softens and he seems to recognize the apprehension in my voice, because he slips his arm under me until I'm resting on his chest.

"Well, I haven't told them yet. I figured it's a little too early still. My mother is going to be ecstatic, because I'm an only child. All her hopes, for grandchildren, lay with me. When I told her about you, I knew she was secretly plotting our wedding arrangements. As for us, I've been thinking too. I definitely make more money doing the traveling gig, so I wanted to know what you thought about me doing that until the baby comes. I can find something more permanent then. It will give us a chance to save some money and maybe find a house that is bigger?"

Even though my whole inside feels like it was squeezed until nothing else was left, my heart is bursting with love.

"That sounds like a plan."

I lift my head and we kiss, no other words are needed.

By the end of the next week, I feel much more confident in my ability to manage my morning sickness. The trick is to sleep in as late as possible and pop a ginger gum in my mouth anytime I feel a wave of nausea. I also learned to be much more secret about being sick at work. Often talking on the phone and hitting the mute button while I vomit into the trash can, under my desk. Picking the conversation up without missing a beat.

The only thing I miss is food! It seems this baby is a health nut. It won't let me eat anything salty, sugary, fried or with any flavor! Yeah, that pretty much cuts out everything I love to eat! Lately, I've been living off of toast and oatmeal. Last night, I dreamt that I went to a buffet that stretched for miles. I woke up drooling on my pillow.

I glance over at the time on my computer screen. There is almost one hour left before I check out to go for my first doctor visit. I already have everything covered for work. Jackie, one of the therapists at the office, will cover the times when I have to leave. She is the only person I've told, besides Noah, Tim and Darcy. Noah is able to arrange his schedule so he can come with me too! Reaching into my purse, I unwrap a ginger gummy and get back to work. Eager to pass the time quickly and get to my appointment.

Noah pulls into the parking lot at the same time as me. We walk hand-in-hand to the OBGYN office. They have a bulletin board hanging on the wall, next to the receptionist window, with babies of all ages in Halloween costumes. No doubt a seasonal display for the upcoming holiday. I spot an infant dressed up as a flower. The head of the baby is surrounded by large white petals and the little body is dressed in a green romper. I point it out to Noah as we wait to get checked in. He chuckles when he sees the image.

"Of course we can dress up our kid in a flower costume. You might lose our baby when it blends in with your planters."

I give him a playful jab, with my elbow, as I step up to the window to fill out paperwork and sign in. Once we get my weight, blood pressure and a urine sample, I change into my gown and wait for the next step. Our doctor comes into the room. He is an older man with glasses and a full head of white hair. His smile puts us both at ease as he shakes our hands and introduces himself as Dr. Lee.

After my exam he asks if we are ready to hear our baby.

"You mean it has a heartbeat already?" I ask, stunned.

For some reason, I was thinking all the morning sickness fuss was due to hormone changes and since I still wasn't showing, there was nothing really developed in there.

He chuckles as he replies, "Well yes, your baby had its own separate heartbeat from you for probably a week or two by now."

Noah looks over at me with a slight frown, "Haven't you been reading those books in the living room?"

Well, honestly, I haven't given them much thought.

"Not really. By the time I get home and settled, I just feel like doing nothing but sleeping. I'll look at them with you tonight. I promise."

Dr. Lee spreads some clear gel on my belly and the room goes quiet. That's when I hear it. The steady heartbeat of my child. It reminds me of a train chugging up a hill fast. I laugh loudly, with joy, as a tear escapes down my cheek. Noah is smiling at me too. He reaches to give my hand a squeeze. Dr. Lee marks some recordings on a paper and wipes my belly off.

"Everything sounds fantastic. You both take care. Before you leave, please schedule your next appointment in a month."

We both thank him as he turns and exits the room.

"Oh my Noah! We just heard our baby, this is so real now! I'll eat oatmeal the whole 9 months if that's what it takes."

"This is pretty cool, Elena. You are doing a great job. Go ahead and get changed. I'll meet you in the waiting room."

He kisses my forehead and leaves the room. As I'm sitting by myself, I reflect on the sound I just heard and rub my stomach. Closing my eyes a thought pops into my head. *I don't have to live in the shadow of my past anymore.*

Opening my eyes, I start to get dressed, reminding myself this office may be similar to the past rooms where many women met a different fate. Today, I leave with the light shining on my face. I won't look back anymore. My past doesn't have to define my future. Slipping on my pants, I think back to the bulletin board in the waiting room. The little babies dressed up in colorful costumes and shuddered at the thought that in my past, a bulletin board for halloween would have fit right in, on the office wall, in our waiting room. All the babies would have been little skeletons.

Just as I promised Noah, I went home and started reading through the pregnancy books. I even downloaded a pregnancy app that gave me daily updates. Every week it gave me a fruit of the week to compare my baby too.

I was now on week 13. My baby was like a peach.

As the days went by, I slowly started to feel like my old self. My appetite came back full force. Noah and I are enjoying eating out again and as he puts it, "putting some weight back on me".

I still don't have any sign of a bump. I do notice that my breasts have already gotten so big. I had to go up a cup size. I'm not the only one to notice, as Noah and I start to take advantage of my energy. We quickly find out that because I'm already pregnant, we don't have to worry about condoms anymore. The sex has been better than ever.

The past couple months I haven't spent that much time with Darcy. On one of the occasions we met up on the porch, I know she was pretty much feeling the same way as me. Coping with the morning sickness and exhaustion.

I shared my tips for getting through the day, and she shared that she was getting by on chocolate milk and jerky sticks. In between work and rest, we both agreed to make some time to hang out. Well, once we started feeling better, anyway. I would definitely have more time soon because

Noah was going to be starting a new contract after Thanksgiving. I wasn't looking forward to that, but I knew I would have Darcy around to keep me company. He was doing this for our family. I would have the rest of our lives to hang out with him. I was glad to have Darcy in my life and that we were going through this together. I hoped our kids would become friends, too.

Darcy

When we get back from our labor day getaway, I'm annoyed by everything. I monitor my body constantly, waiting for any sign that I might be getting my period. Hoping this was all just a false-positive, on the test. When I go to the bathroom, I sometimes wipe twice, checking the toilet paper for any sign of a pink tint to my urine. A sign my cycle will be starting.

Finally, I decided to get a second opinion, to calm my nerves. I want to know for certain. I called my primary doctor and made an appointment. After I provide a urine sample, I wait in the room pacing back and forth. My doctor comes in and his smile already tells me everything I need to know.

"Congratulations, Darcy. You are pregnant!"

I give him a weak smile back and thank him for his time. I assure him I will get set up with an OBGYN and start taking prenatals. Now that I know for sure this is really happening, the whole idea seems so scary. For the next month, I choose to stay busy and take time to myself to process this. Tim senses I'm adjusting, and even though I know he is thrilled, he gives me space. He starts helping with house chores, even though I take the dishes out after he falls asleep and redo them. Just to make sure they are done right.

By the time October rolls around, my self-inflicted terrible mood is completely hijacked by my pregnancy hormones. They like to make me miserable. Leaving me completely exhausted each day with a side of bonus nausea.

Speaking with Elena, I know she has been vomiting pretty much every day. I wish my morning sickness was like that. Instead, I constantly feel like I have to puke, but everytime I try nothing comes up. It reminds me when I drink too much and I stick my fingers down my throat because I know I'm going to throw up sooner or later. I might as well get it over with so I can start to feel better. I've tried that and nothing happens, other than I scratch my throat. I never feel any better. Not only that but everything just tastes off. I'm left craving chocolate milk and jerky sticks. Things I would never buy any other time.

As I came home one day after work, I threw my stuff down on the kitchen table and headed to the fridge. I'm trying to find something that appeals to me. As I grab a yogurt, Tim is standing there with a nervous face. I know this face. He usually wears it when he has been thinking about asking me something for a long time and has finally got the courage to come to me.

"So, I was wondering when you plan on seeing a doctor. I know Elena and Noah already went and got checked out."

I'm frowning at him, "Well, Tim, maybe I don't want to see a doctor. You already know that I went through something in high school. I really dont feel like spending money on a stupid copay just to have someone to defile me and say, 'yep, you're pregnant'. I already know this! I'm not an idiot. I went to school for this. Believe me, I know what I'm doing here. I don't want to see a doctor. It's just a waste of time anyway. I could probably deliver this baby here, at home, by myself, if I wanted to. When the time comes, we will just go to the hospital. I'll have the baby and then we go on with our lives."

I wanted to eat that yogurt, but now I've lost my appetite. Normally, I dont raise my voice at Tim. We rarely argue. I'm just so overwhelmed. Tim would normally retreat now, and leave me alone. Instead, he pulls out one of the kitchen chairs and sits down. Maybe, by sitting, he is trying to seem smaller and less threatening. He could also be letting me know he wants to finish this conversation.

"I'm not really sure what happened to you in high school. I hope one day you can come to me with that. I understand it was traumatic. I'm just worried about your health and the health of our baby. I know you have been taking some time to adjust. I'm seriously so happy for this news. I'm not going anywhere. I want to help you and make this work. You are not alone."

His last words break me; like dynamite being thrown at the wall I've built around my emotions. I try to blink back tears as he stands up and slowly walks towards me. By the time he reaches me, everything breaks free and bursts out of me. I fall into his arms as all the fear and anxiety from the past month slowly leaves my body. I stand there sobbing in his embrace until the light fades from the window and we are left in the dark.

Tim and I have come to a compromise, after that night in the kitchen. Instead of going to see a doctor, I monitor my own vitals at home. I promise him I will go to the hospital if I think anything is wrong. Noah lent Tim some of the pregnancy care books and he has been reading through them every morning, before work, to learn about our baby's development. Soon he is updating me on my progress and seems to know just as much about how to care for an infant as he does for his fantasy characters in his game. I'm very impressed. When he suggests we meet with a midwife he found online, I agree. We scheduled a visit with her for the end of October.

I took a half day off on the afternoon of our first visit with our midwife so I could get home and clean up. We rarely have visitors and I wanted to make sure everything was in its place. When I pull in, I see Elena is already home. She is on the porch hanging fake spider webs and big, black spiders covered in faux fur.

"Hey what's going on? Are we having a party I wasn't aware of?"

She looks back from her step ladder and gives me a big smile.

"Hey! No, I was getting ready for the trick or treaters tomorrow. It was slow in the office, so a therapist covered for me this afternoon. I took some personal time."

She steps down from the ladder and we meet up on the front porch steps. It's a surprisingly warm day and it feels nice to sit for a second, in the sun, and smell the crisp fall air.

"So how have you been feeling? Still eating those jerky sticks or is your appetite back?"

Catching a piece of stray spider web, I rub it between my fingertips.

"Actually, I've been feeling great lately. The morning sickness is almost gone and Tim has been so cool with everything. We actually meet with our midwife today. That's why I came home early – so I could clean up. How have you been doing?"

Elena stretches back smiling, "Starting to feel like normal. I've been getting my energy back. The only good thing to come out of this month are these." She puts her hands to her side and does a little shimmy showing off her chest. We both laugh. "Now you've got some competition, Darcy. Let's see who will get the biggest belly! So what's a midwife do?"

"Well, basically, Tim and I don't really want to do the whole gyno thing. We want something all natural and a midwife is trained to help with pregnancy and delivery. Plus, with my nursing background, I feel okay with being able to recognize any signs of trouble."

Elena is listening intently, "That's so cool. We already started seeing a doctor and are pretty comfortable with him. I'd totally do what you are doing, but without Noah around later on, I just feel better with being checked up in the hospital."

"Yeah I get that. Well, I have to get going. I miss hanging out. Maybe we can get together soon and do some clothes shopping? I may beat you in the belly competition. I already feel like my pants are getting tight!"

We stand up together and Elena pulls me in for a hug, "Of course, buddy. Talk to you soon. Don't worry, I'll take care of the trick or treaters tomorrow so we don't get TP'd. Noah and I will be handing out candy. Maybe I'll leave some out for you."

Unlocking my front door and opening it up I turn, "Oh, yes! Anything chocolate would be great! See ya."

It was nice to see Elena. I feel so fortunate to be going through this at the same time as her. She is going to be such a lifesaver during this pregnancy. I can already feel it.

THE SECOND TRIMESTER

Elena

Flipping through my book, I have to read the page over again because I couldn't focus on the words. In the seat next to me, Noah is already sleeping. We are currently halfway through our flight to Omaha. We are spending the week with Noah's family, for Thanksgiving. Too distracted by my thoughts, I put the book away and looked out my window, watching the clouds float by. This week there is so much going on. Not only did I reach my second trimester milestone, but Noah and I will share our news with his family. Then, when we fly back, on Friday, he will be packing and getting ready to leave for his next contract. He will be in Detroit for 3 months.

Last night, while we packed, Noah was talking about all the family members I would be meeting. From his mom and dad to his aunts and uncles. I sat on the bed and listened to all the different personalities and quirks. He described them and he expressed his excitement in having them all meet me and learn about our news. I know he assures me they will embrace me as their own. That I'll be part of the family too.

It still feels crappy that I can't share this news with my grandmother. Other than her, I don't really have anyone left to call family. My grandmother immigrated from Mexico when she was young. She didn't really talk about her early years. I know she had my mother when she was about 20. My grandfather died unexpectedly, in a work accident, leaving her heartbroken. She never remarried. She found a steady job, as a greenhouse worker, until she retired to take care of me. That must be where I got my love of plants from.

Growing up, I had Thanksgiving dinner sitting at the little table in my grandmother's kitchen. We would hold hands and say prayers, just the two of us and the little rotisserie chicken. We never got a turkey. It would have been too much meat for just us.

In college, I took shifts around campus doing work that nobody else wanted to do because they had plans for the holidays or family obligations they had to attend. I always felt sad and jealous during those times. I guess the best thing to come out of this new relationship, with Noah, is that our child would never have to experience that. They would always have family gatherings and lots of hugs and kisses from relatives that have missed them and love them.

Rubbing my small bump, I feel that is what I can be most thankful for this week, besides Noah, of course. I look over at him sleeping and smile. Picking up my book again, I'm able to find the words. I decided this is going to be a great week.

Noah's Mother is waiting for us at the baggage claim. I recognize her from the pictures Noah has shared of his family. She is wearing a bright orange cardigan and has her graying, brown hair braided down to the side. It is laying over her shoulder and it bounces up and down as she jumps with joy when she catches sight of Noah.

She says, "Hey, you guys," as she wraps her arms around him.

He rolls his eyes, but I know he is secretly loving this. Who wouldn't be? I'm standing next to him holding the handle to my suitcase, when she lets him go and faces me.

"Elena, sweetheart, I've heard so much about you!" She winks at Noah while speaking to me. "You are the one who has captured my sweet boy's heart. I know you must be pretty special. Just as much as you are beautiful."

With this, she pulls me in for a hug. I feel the same amount of love she just showed Noah. I hug back. Here is another reason to be thankful… a mothers love for me.

All my worries melt away as I get to know Noah's family. I love all of them. I feel so welcome. His cousin, Mary, and I are about the same age. We quickly find out that we both have a passion for jigsaw puzzles. We spent the afternoon working on a huge flower garden scene, in the downstairs family room. I love how effortlessly everyone gets along.

The next day, for Thanksgiving, I wake with my stomach growling. The aroma of turkey baking is already filling the house. After setting up the table and making sure everyone had a plate and silverware, Noah's father stands up to say the prayer. Closing my eyes and bowing my head reminds me of the prayers my grandmother would say over our dinners. I quickly feel a pang of regret when I realize I actually haven't prayed in years. Breaking a promise I made to her when I moved out.

After I say amen, with everyone, I also make a promise to myself that I will start praying again soon and make the same tradition with my child. I'll have time for that later though. I'm starving now! Just as I'm about to dig into my food, Noah stands up, at the table, and I realize it's going to happen now. He raises up his glass.

"I would like to just say something I'm thankful for before we start. I'm thankful to be able to make it home and spend these couple days with all of you. I'm thankful that this year I met Elena and she has changed my life. It will only get better because next year we are bringing another person to the table." Looking at his mother now. "Mom, you will need to fit a high chair somewhere, because our guest will be a tad small for these chairs."

At this last part, his mothers eyes grow wide. All at once it seems the room is filled with squeals of delight, misty eyes and I'm getting hugged by three people at once. Noah is still standing, looking over me with the biggest smile and the proudest eyes. I'm glad I chose a roomy dress to wear. Not only because my pants are all getting too tight, but also because everyone made me take extra on my plate. I'm thoroughly stuffed.

Later that night, after all the excitement had waned and the food was put away, Noah and I lay spooning in his old bedroom. The tryptophan from the turkey lulled me to sleep. I couldn't help but smile and tick off the list in my head of all I had to be thankful for.

Darcy

Stepping out of the house, I pull the wheels of my suitcase up, so they go over the threshold of my front door. Tim is right behind me, with his bag. He is locking up while I walk to the car. I've been dreading this trip home for Thanksgiving. Tim and I made a deal when we got married that I had to go home and visit every other year for the holidays. So Yippee… this was the year I had to go home and pretend to be happy. To be so interested in everyone blah blah blah… I already have the trip planned. We get to Tim's parents tonight. Then we'll have Thanksgiving with his family at 12 and Thanksgiving with my family at 5. Then we stay there for the night and head home first thing Friday morning. I recline my chair back and try to sleep for the drive home, sad that the only thing missing from this trip would be any form of alcohol.

The nice thing about Tim's house is I can usually slip away unnoticed and watch old westerns with his dad, in the den. His father likes to prop his legs up in his favorite recliner. Nobody usually bothers him as he can be known to be quite grumpy. Although, I think this is just a ruse to keep his overexcitable wife and children at arm's length. I can only stand being around them for a short time. Tim's mother sometimes reminds me of one of those little jack russell dogs who just run around excited all day long. Tim and his sister must have inherited that gene from her, as they are now in the kitchen making cookies and chatting incessantly. I don't know how this man survived growing up with them and their constant cheeriness. We have a mutual respect for each other. We both like our space and the peace and quiet.

The next morning goes the same way, until Tim comes in to let us know everything is ready. Annoyed because I was actually getting into this scene, I reluctantly get up to go eat. Of course, the table is set up like the cover of a magazine and I don't understand all the fuss. One year Tim and I made chicken nuggets and macaroni and cheese for Thanksgiving. Tim tried to make a turkey, but by dinner time, the thing was still raw in the middle. We gave up on that. He is horrible at cooking and I lack the motivation to actually try. Plus, all the dishes and food just doesn't make sense for two people.

Tim's father puts his hands together to say grace. Tim suddenly interrupts him. His father raises an eyebrow, at him, as if to say this better be good.

"Sorry to cut you off, Dad. I was hoping to say the prayer this time. Lord, thank you for this time with family and the wonderful dinner we have prepared. Bless it and nourish us, Amen. I also want to just say Darcy and I have some news to share with you."

Holy crap! I thought we both agreed to not share this in person. That he would do it over the phone. I should have known he wouldn't be able to wait. He would want to do this in person so his mother could freak out and baby him the rest of the trip. It takes all I have not to roll my eyes or give away my annoyed feelings. I smile and wait for Tim to finish his announcement.

At this, he pulls up his hoodie to reveal a t-shirt with the words, *I Put a Turkey in that Oven, Roasting until next year,* with an arrow pointing in my direction. Of course leave it to him to announce our pregnancy with a stupid t-shirt. Here. It. Comes.

His mother is jumping up from the table and hugging us, while his sister comes to my other side squeezing me.

Even his father is smiling, "Congratulations to you both! I'm so happy for you."

Okay. Maybe I do feel a little bit happy. Maybe that's why Tim's father avoids them... because all this energy is kinda catchy. I can't help but smile as Tim reaches under the table and gives my hand a reassuring squeeze. I squeeze him back, to let him know all is forgiven and I'm not mad. After we are given one final hug, his mother reluctantly lets us leave so we can head to my parents house with promises we will keep her updated every week.

On the short drive over to my childhood home, I remind Tim that my parents probably won't find any humor in his shirt so I'll just make the announcement. I know he is probably disappointed he won't get to use his shirt again, but he doesn't say anything because he doesn't want to push the subject. I think he realized he wasn't supposed to have said anything to his parents to begin with.

Pulling into the driveway, I feel my chest tighten upon being back home. I always dread being back here. No matter the amount of trees surrounding me, this place always feels like the air is thicker. I can never quite breathe in enough oxygen. The only thing to look forward to will be a nice quiet dinner. My brother is spending the day with his wife in West Virginia. My sister and her husband decided to have Thanksgiving on their own this year. They wanted to spend the holidays together in their new house, "To break it in" as she referred to it, on the phone this week.

My mother and father already have the food set up. My father is carving the turkey as we come in. My mother is laying down silverware. I notice there is no tablecloth. She already Tim-proofed this meal, I see. Dinner is almost over and I think I can get away with it when Tim clears his throat and looks over at me expectedly. Ugh. Might as well get this over with before he grows impatient and shows the shirt.

"So, Tim and I wanted to let you both know we are expecting our first child next Spring."

I know this announcement seemed weird but so is the idea of having a baby. So yeah, I guess that will have to do. My mother brings her hands together in a prayer position in front of her face.

"Oh my, that is great news Darcy!"

My father slaps Tim on the shoulder, "Congratulations to you both."

Now Tim is beaming, "Yep, we just told my parents too. We are both very happy."

I quickly put on a smile to match his. Pretending is easy when you go back to the place where you learned how to do it best.

After I've finished helping my mother dry the dishes and everything is put back, I steal away to the front porch, grabbing my hoodie. I sit on the porch swing to think about everything that has happened during the day. I wonder how Elena is doing and if she had to go through all this attention today. I know Noah was planning on telling his family while they were there. I'm in the middle of thinking how nice it must be that Elena doesn't have to worry about sharing this news with anyone and living up to their expectations, when my mother steps out on the porch looking for me.

"Hey. There you are. I was looking for you."

Walking over she pulls her cardigan front pieces together closing the gap in the middle.

I ask, "Do you need help with anything else?"

As she is sitting down next to me, I turn to face her.

"Oh no. Thank you for all your help cleaning up. I just wanted to… um… well. I just wanted to talk to you about your big news. While we cleaned, it got me thinking and I just wanted to say, I'm so proud of you. I know you don't like the attention. I try to make sure I never make a fuss over you, but you have really turned out to be quite the young woman. I'm honored you took after me and became a nurse. Tim talks about how all your patients love you so much and you even house sit for one. I can't say I have the same bedside manner. Not even as a mother. It was always hard for me to connect and I apologize for that. I tried the best I could. Anyways, I'm just so happy with this news and I know you will make the best mother."

She pats my knee and smiles at me. I find that I'm sitting entirely still; listening to her every word as if I'm an explorer coming out of the desert and finding a fresh spring. I don't chug down this conversation. Instead, I take small sips savoring every last word. My mother has never been so open like this with me. I'm left wondering if the reason she has always seemed standoffish was because she thought that's what I wanted. Maybe I've always pushed her away. Even more so after the incident without even realizing I was doing it. Neither of us say anything else. I feel something change in our relationship and I reach down and squeeze her hand on my knee. If the last time I was pregnant I drove us apart, I know this time this baby is going to bring us together.

Elena

Standing in the driveway, I watch until Noah's car turns the corner and I can no longer see him. Unwillingly, I walk back to the house. It's still dark out. I should go back to sleep, but I know I'll probably just toss and turn. Anyway, I decide to watch tv for a little bit. Noah is on his way to his next contract and will be gone for about twelve weeks. I won't see him until Christmas when we both fly to Omaha, to spend the holiday with his parents.

In the meantime, I plan on keeping busy with work and hanging out with Darcy. We made plans to do some clothes shopping and have lunch. The perfect way to spend a Sunday. I'm still not used to this chilly weather. Contrary to what Darcy thinks about me moving here straight from Texas, I've actually been living in this state for the past 10 years.

I decide to grab a blanket from the closet, to snuggle up with, on the couch. As I'm pulling down a big sherpa lined flannel blanket, it falls into my arms. At the same time, my sight catches on the box tucked away behind it. I let out a small shriek, forgetting I had put it there months ago, in an attempt to hide it from Noah. Closing my eyes and letting out a big sigh, I know I should probably let him know about that soon. Definitely before our baby is born. The best thing to do would be to come clean about my past and let all my secrets out, but I'm just not ready. I don't want to deal with it now. Instead, I grab some beach towels and throw them in front of it, hiding it from view and my mind for a while.

Not only does December bring merry tunes and blinking lights, my round little belly finally pops out. Like some kind of homage to Santa, my baby doesn't want to be left behind. I'm so glad for the maternity clothes I bought with Darcy. Turning side-to-side, in the bathroom mirror, there is officially the start of my little bump. I snap a picture and send it to Noah and Darcy. Week 16, an avocado, according to my pregnancy app. To some, it might just look like I'm bloated. I know there is a little person in there, just hanging out. Maybe that's why it hasn't been so bad since Noah has been gone. I'm no longer alone.

When I open the office, one of my favorite things to do is plug in the lights for the Christmas tree. I decided not to do anything with the house because I wouldn't even be there for Christmas. I've also been saving up all my extra money, for when the baby comes.

When I arrive at work it puts me into the holiday spirit. I can glance from my desk, and see the lights blinking in the corner. I was the one to decorate everything. I took an hour after work last week, after everyone had left, to put on christmas music and hang the lights. The bulbs were cheap plastic ones. I hung them as if they were crystal. I haven't put up a tree since I was living in Texas, with my grandmother. The task makes me feel closer to her and my childhood.

Shaking my head to break from the thoughts of my past, I turn my attention back to the present. I get to work turning the lights on, in the rest of the office, and prepare myself for the busy day. It seems like the office has never been busier. I heard a therapist say the other day that the holidays can be the hardest for people who don't have anyone to celebrate with. I nodded, in agreement, because I used to be one of those people. I'm so grateful I have a family to go home to this year. During my lunch break I check out flights to Omaha. While I'm looking at times for arrival, I send a quick text to Noah with an idea.

> Sooo... There is actually a flight that arrives in Omaha on the 22nd at 11am. Do you think you can fit that into your schedule instead of the later flight we had talked about? Your parents would still be at work and we could fit in some "alone" time before they come back. ☺

His reply is immediate. Ha!

Oh, I can fit that into my schedule for sure! Can't wait to see you! ☺

Smiling, I put my phone away and click confirm on my flight. Then I send a quick text to Darcy telling her I'm picking up dinner for the night and I'd be stopping over.

After work, I stop at the Thai restaurant that we love and get our favorite meals to go. When I walk into her place, with the bags in hand, I see Darcy sitting, on the couch, having an animated conversation about her plans for Christmas. She motions with her hand, to me, she will just be another minute.

"Okay, Mom. I have to go. Elena is here with our food. Okay. yeah you too. Bye."

What?! As I take off my scarf and put my stuff in the closet, I'm surprised that she was talking to her mother. Not just that she was talking to her, but that she's talking in such an easygoing way.

"So how is your mother?"

Darcy comes over to greet me and help carry the stuff to the table.

"Well, she actually called with a great idea. Joint baby showers, at her house, in the beginning of April? What do you think!"

I grab some forks and meet her at the table.

"Wow, that's so considerate of her. Are you sure you want to share that special day with me?"

Darcy already has a mouthful of some of the appetizer but she is shaking her head up and down excitedly, swallowing her food.

"Of course, Elena. We are doing this whole thing together. Why not a baby shower too? My mom and I have been talking a lot more since I was home for Thanksgiving. She is super psyched about her first grandbaby.

Oh! guess what else?! Tim told me last night that he got a new job as a manager in a restaurant in town!"

Now, I'm swallowing my food down fast.

"That's fantastic news Darcy! All of it! I'm so glad you are talking with your mom more. Wow! I mean Tim being a manager… it seems so grown up for him."

Darcy rolls her eyes, "I know, but I guess he told me since he is going to be a dad, he wants to make sure he isn't still delivering pizzas when the baby comes."

"Very cool. So are you guys going home for Christmas this year?"

Grabbing a napkin and wiping her mouth, she replies, "Yes we will leave on the 23rd, after work, and spend time with both of our families."

Pausing before my next bite I reply, "Cool. I actually just booked my flight for Omaha today, at work. I'll leave the day before you."

"That's great. My schedule is pretty busy, so I might not be home at my normal time the rest of the month. If you need anything, just text me, okay? I hope you have a great time with Noah and his family."

Smiling, I think back to our first time eating Thai. I'm grateful for how far our friendship has come since then. I'm glad to see this side of Darcy. I know the rest of our pregnancy will only bring us closer.

As I wait at the baggage claim, I keep an eye out for my luggage, and also, Noah. The belt turns the corner and I grab my suitcase. It's easy to spot, with its bright floral pattern. It was a gift from Noah when we flew out last month.

Turning around, I see him walking towards me and I stand waiting for him to reach me. He pulls me in, for a hug, and then reaches up with both hands and holds my face as he says hello with a long, tender kiss. Pulling back, my legs feel wobbly.

"Wow, I missed you too, sweetheart. How was your flight?"

He reaches out and takes my suitcase. I'm left carrying my purse and he is pulling both carry-ons.

"It went slow. I'm excited to finally see you. I think this may be the only time I can say you look like you are getting a belly and not get slapped for it."

Laughing and slapping his shoulder playfully I respond, "Yeah this is the only time I'll take it as a compliment."

While saying this my hands rub my belly. I wore a tight shirt so he could actually see how much it's grown since our last time together. We are now week 18. Our baby is as big as a sweet potato. As I wait for him to bring the rental car around and pick me up, I send a quick text to Darcy. I don't want to forget in the midst of all the busy holiday plans, and time hanging out with Noah.

> Hey Buddy, I just wanted to let you know, I got here safe. Noah and I are on the way to his parents. Have a Merry Christmas! I'll see you when I get back! Enjoy this time away from me because the next couple months you won't be able to get rid of me. Ha! xoxo

I see the little check that the message was read but there is no reply. Huh… that's strange. I don't think too much about it. Noah is pulling the car up to the curb, when I feel it for the first time. It's like a butterfly turning in my belly. Putting my hand to my belly quickly and opening my mouth in disbelief, at Noah, who has come around to open the door for me.

"I think I just felt the baby move, Noah!"

He reaches out and puts his hand on my belly. Nothing happens.

"Hmm… maybe when it gets a little bigger you can feel it?"

He gives me a quick hug before I get in the car. Little did I know, at that time, miles away, while I was feeling my baby's first movements, Darcy was already planning my last ones.

Darcy

For the first time in a long time, I feel free. No longer held by the constraints of my past. All my guilt and doubt lift up to the sky and float away like stray balloons after a child's birthday party. Elena has started to show lately. I feel like my belly is almost twice her size! My wardrobe consisted of baggy clothes and loose fitting scrubs before I was pregnant, but I decided to order some maternity scrubs anyway. I'm inside unpacking the artificial christmas tree, when I hear the thud of the package, as it's dropped off on my front porch.

I don't care for Christmas nor new clothes, but here I am eager to decorate and inspect my new maternity wardrobe. Tim comes out of the kitchen, as I bring the box in. He hurriedly comes to my side and takes it from me. It's been like that ever since I started to show. He is attentive to my needs. He is reading pregnancy books. The best news yet, was yesterday, when he came home to let me know he was applying for a job as restaurant manager. He is hoping to leave his job as a pizza delivery driver. I mean how cool is that? Plus, ever since Thanksgiving, I've actually been calling my mother back when I know I won't lose a signal. Everyone is so excited for this baby and all the support they are throwing behind us is making me feel like I can do this. It's like magic growing inside of me, giving me everything that I wanted for my future. Reassuring me that everything is going to be okay. The past has worked itself out.

"Hey, I got you something at the mall yesterday."

I glance over at Tim, who is holding a small box. Opening it, I found a glass christmas tree ornament. The silhouette of a pregnant woman on the front with the words *presents for two please*. I laugh out loud. I know Tim probably wanted this on a shirt, but I would never wear it, so he opted for this instead. Reaching over, I squeeze his hand.

"I love it, thanks Tim."

It's the first thing to go on the tree when we have it set up. We sit down to watch the lights while we enjoy a cup of hot chocolate. For the first time in our entire relationship, I fall asleep in his arms and have dreams coated in sugar and snowflakes.

Pulling up my new blue maternity scrubs, my phone buzzes on the bathroom counter. It's a picture from Elena. She is showing me her bump. We started doing this a couple weeks ago. Amazed by the difference, in our growing bellies, I take a quick pic and send it back. Week 16 and our babies are the size of an avocado. My bump feels more like a cantaloupe. Maybe I'll win the biggest belly competition after all.

The month is flying by. Tim and I make plans to go back to our hometown for the holidays. My schedule is full and it seems every time I see a patient they load me up with food to take home or presents for the baby. I've even got some hand knit baby hats from some of the women I see. I promise to take pictures and show them when the baby comes. I'm in the drive thru waiting for a coffee, when Elena texts me letting me know she is getting Thai and will be over later. Sweet! I've been so hungry lately. That sounds delicious. I quickly text her back a drooly face and thumbs up.

Later that day, I get home before Elena and take the time to call my mom back. She called earlier and left a voicemail about something she wanted to discuss with me. It turns out, she had the idea of throwing a baby shower, at our church, back home in April. She wanted to check with me first before doing any planning. I insist it's a great idea and suggest we also do one for Elena because she really doesn't have family. She is a great friend. My mother is delighted with the idea. Just as we are wrapping up the conversation, Elena comes in the door with the food.

I can tell she is a little surprised by my conversation with my mom. In a way, so am I. It's been a while since Elena and I got to sit down to talk. I tell her about all the good news. The baby shower in April and Tim getting the restaurant manager job. He will be working at the pizza shop while he trains at the new restaurant, before he takes over in January. So we won't see each other hardly at all this month. We leave on the 23rd to go home but that's fine with me. I'm just happy at all the effort he is putting into everything. Elena and I hug goodbye and she promises to text when she gets off the plane. After I get everything cleaned up, from dinner, and I'm settled in bed, for the night, I think back to the first time Elena and I had Thai. I was so hesitant to go. In the end, I decided why not. Look at the way everything turned out.

Opening up the medicine cabinet, I root around, looking for something I can take that would be safe for this backache that's been bothering me all night. Yesterday, I must have pulled something when I lugged a bag of old clothes to Tim's car. He was going to drop them off at the thrift shop. He was upset that I couldn't wait for him to get out of the shower, but I was in a cleaning mood and it was in the way. I figured what was the harm. All night, I had a steady pain. Tim offered to take me to the hospital but I dismissed his worry and told him I would be fine.

It looks like the safe painkiller I have is acetaminophen. Shutting my cabinet door, my phone buzzes on the sink. It's from Elena. She is sending her Monday update on her bump. We are now at 18 weeks. Not in the mood for a pic, I just send her a smiley face back.

Going into the kitchen, I'm looking at my options for breakfast. Nothing appeals to me. My mouth starts to water and I think I'm going to throw up. I take a couple crackers and my water bottle and lay down on the couch hoping it will subside. I have some personal time that I still haven't used, so I text my office manager and let her know I will be taking the day off. I was around a patient last week who had just got over the stomach bug. All weekend, I felt tired like I was coming down with something. This is probably the beginning of the symptoms. If I'm going to start vomiting all day, I want to be home. I text Tim to let him know and immediately he insists he should come home. I promise him that I will be okay and I know how to take care of myself. He won't be home until late, while he is transitioning from having two jobs to just one. I expect to have some peace and quiet for the day.

Just as I suspected, around lunch time, I'm feeling worse. I moved to the bedroom so I could be closer to the bathroom. I've been having to go constantly. I make sure to drink plenty of water and try to keep eating crackers, even though my stomach is in knots. Eventually, it seems there is nothing else left in me and I feel sweaty and gross.

I decide to take a bath and freshen up and maybe that will also help this cramping in my back. I pop in a couple more acetaminophen and try to let the warm water soothe my achy body and calm my crampy stomach. Laying with my head on a wrapped towel, I settle back, listening to some soft rock. I let the water lap around my body and try to relax as my pain feels like it's getting tighter in my back. I open my eyes slightly as I shift toward my side. I feel like I'm in a daze. I'm confused, as my hand reaches out to touch the water. It takes a minute for my brain and body to communicate that I'm moving my hand through red water. Something is wrong.

Sitting up fast, I'm raked by a sharp pain in my side that makes me double over. Where did all this blood come from? It seems to dawn on me too late. The pain in the side. The upset stomach. The cramping I mistaked for a stomach virus. I'm having a miscarriage. There is nothing I can do to stop it.

All at once, another sharp pain crashes through my body. I pull my knees to my chest as I close my eyes and swallow down vomit. The tears start to come as I plead, "Please no. Please no." Wringing the towel with my hands, the sharp cramps and bloody water are a sharp contrast to the soft love song playing. Just as I start to think this is the end and I'm feeling horrible that Tim will have to find me like this, the pain starts to subside. I loosen my grip on the towel and my body starts to relax. Sitting up slowly, I can now see clumps of tissue. Floating near my ankle is the perfectly formed body of my baby.

Blinking back tears now, I wish I had died before. I wish I didn't have to see this image or have to deal with this. How am I supposed to tell everyone? How do I tell Tim and our family? I lean my head back and sob. Still sobbing, I reach down and let the water out. My hopes and dreams swirling and disappearing forever down the drain.

I take the little body and wrap it in a clean towel. I do this fast so I don't have to look long. The image is already seared into my mind. Kind of like when you look at a bright light and then close your eyes. There is a faint outline still there fading slowly. However, everytime I close my eyes, I see the white outline of my child. My legs are shaking as I try to stand. I need to clean this before anyone sees what has happened. I need time to process this and figure out what to do next. The first thing I do is go right to the extra strength painkillers. No need to avoid them now. I pop in double the recommended amount. What is it going to do to me anyway? I'm already broken inside.

Throwing the last of the cleaning rags away, the bathroom sparkles back at me. A reassurance letting me know it holds my secret. Nobody will ever know what we went through together. I've taken my baby and tenderly wrapped it in gauze. I put the little body in a frozen fruit bag in the back of the freezer. I dumped all the fruit out. It was part of my healthy eating diet, for my pregnancy. I doubt I'll be having any smoothies anytime soon. That seems to be the best place, until I can find the words to let Tim know.

He already texted me earlier to check up on me and all I could do was give him a thumbs up and let him know I was feeling better. Crawling into bed, I pull the covers over my head. With heavy eyes, from crying, I let the exhaustion take me over.

When Tim gets home that night, I can't bear to say anything. I tell him I have a stomach bug and it would be best to sleep on the couch. Afraid of my germs and the chance of ruining our trip home for Christmas, he doesn't seem to argue. I cancel all my patients for the rest of the week and claim my personal hours. A first for me to actually use them before they run out.

After a couple days, I start to feel some of my strength returning. I can finally eat some toast and drink the tea Tim has left out for me, on the bed stand. We are supposed to leave for our trip tomorrow. I just don't know if I can do this. I'll have to tell Tim tonight. He can call our families, with the news, and we can stay home. It's not going to be much of a Christmas this year.

A nagging feeling of guilt has been bumping around in my head today. I can't help but wonder if the reason I lost this baby was because of my abortion. I never did feel right about the way it went down. How the doctor seemed to rush through everything. Maybe she has lost her medical license.

I pull out my laptop to look up her old office. They probably have been slapped with some kind of medical malpractice suit for their sloppy execution, in the office. I'm sure of it. This is all their fault. It has to be.

When I search for the name of that doctor, the website for the clinic is the first thing to pop up. No news stories or headlines about malpractice. I feel defeated. Clicking open the website, I figure why not pour salt on my open wounds. I scroll down through the happy faces of the doctor and her nurses. Then my finger freezes. My eyes glue to the screen. I blink, but the image is still there, unchanged.

I don't understand. Why is Elena on this website? As I look closer, it says Maria Elena. There is no mistaking it. This is my Elena. I click on her name. At the top of the web page, there is a notation that the site was revised a year ago. It obviously has not been updated since. Reading through her work background, it says Maria is the office manager for the clinic, and fundraiser manager. This can't be.

I searched my web browser using this new name and I found a news article dated two years ago with a smiling Elena. She is holding a big fake check for $10,000 written out to the clinic. The headline states *Local Women's clinic raises $10,000 in funds from dinner fundraiser.*

I quickly close the tabs and slam my laptop down so hard I think I heard something crack. I don't care. My thoughts are white hot and I think if she were to walk in this door right now, I would take this laptop and throw it at her head. It wasn't only the doctor doing malpractice that caused this. It was also having my best friend lying to me and pretending this whole time. I know there is no way she would have been at the clinic when I was there. She might as well have been. Taking the torch from her predecessor, she led the way for other foolish women to open their pocketbooks and give out blood money. She might as well have been the one to raise the money that killed my baby the first time. Then maybe today I would be on my way to having a second child. That has to be the reason. Losing my baby is my penance for what I did.

Yet, Elena gets to have it all. Her perfect healthy baby that she gets to deliver. I'll have to see it everyday as she parades it around in front of me with no cares in the world. This is so unfair.

Fighting back the tears, I feel my anger start to transform into frustration. I stop and think. A plan coming into focus, slowly. Just then, my phone pings and I jump, brushing off my thoughts. They come back searing into my head with full intensity. The anger is taking shape. A plan is materializing. Redemption is coming to fruition. There is nothing I can do to shake it this time.

As I read the text from Elena that she has made it safely, I take the phone and hurl it across the room. It smashes against the kitchen wall and lands with a satisfying thud. I only wish I had another to throw. Then, the thought comes back again. This time I won't dismiss it. I let it start to take root in my head. The plan comes into focus. She is the reason I lost my baby. Now, I'm going to be the reason she loses hers. Except it's not her baby that's going to die, it's going to be her.

Elena

Returning home from the trip to Nebraska, I'm feeling renewed. I got to spend time with Noah and I had an amazing time with his family. It was almost like something out of a movie. Growing up in a small household, I know my grandmother did the best she could for me. I wouldn't trade her for anything in the world, but there were times I wished I had a big family like my friends at school.

After college, I had dated. I didn't find anyone that I felt a strong connection to. With Noah, it's like he is the missing piece I've been searching for. While we were saying our goodbyes, at the airport, he whispered into my ear, "I love you."

I couldn't say it back though, not yet. Saying it out loud makes me scared. If I acknowledge it, something bad will happen. Sometimes, I wonder if he is a dream and I'll wake up with a romance novel in my hands.

A reflection of light catches on the brightly colored beads of my bracelet, serving as a reminder of reality. The bright colors of the beads made me gasp when Noah gifted it to me on Christmas. He had explained when he saw the bracelet he knew it was perfect for me because it represented the colors I had brought to his life. Before we met, he was living in black and white.

When I get home I notice the soil in my planters are all dry. Hmm, that's strange. I thought Darcy said she would be over to water them. As I'm thinking about this, I realize Darcy didn't respond to my texts the entire time I was gone. Her car was there when I pulled in, so I grabbed the little gift I had bought for her, from my suitcase, and knocked on her door.

When she opens the door, she is wearing one of Tim's baggy hoodies and some loose fitting joggers. Her face seems thinner. Her eyes have big bags under them. She has a pale appearance, as if she has been sick. I'm immediately concerned and she notices and steps back as if I'm the contagious one.

"Darcy, are you okay?!"

She is still holding on to the door and I can't tell what is going on in her head. I feel like we are back to when we first met. Her guard is up and I have no idea why.

"I've had a stomach bug for the past week. Tim and I actually canceled going home. I've been off work trying to recover. I must have gotten it from one of my patients. I'm slowly getting better. Don't worry."

She says the last words almost as if im the one who caused this or wanted it to happen.

"Well, okay. Let me know if you need anything. I hope this makes you feel better."

Reaching out the small gift she begrudgingly takes it. Unwrapping it, there is a little romper with the words *Buddies, Just like our moms*.

"I have a matching one for my little one."

Her face doesn't change as she fingers the fabric. At last, she looks up and puts on a forced smile.

"Thank you. Well, I better go lay back down. I'll talk to you later."

At this, she closes the door and I'm left standing there alone, confused and hurt. Going back into my house I sit and try to figure out what's going on. She is probably upset because her plans for Christmas got ruined and she doesn't want to hear about how much fun I had. Plus, she looks horrible and is probably feeling like crap. She can be a little socially awkward and often takes her annoyance out on others. I've seen her do it with Tim before. Oh well, I don't take it too personally.

Finishing up my unpacking, I go into the kitchen, to make a snack. While I'm there, I decide to start watering my plants. I begin with the wooden planter I have placed against the wall beside the back door. I'm surprised to find this one is already watered. There are a couple pieces of potting soil behind it, on the floor. Maybe Darcy was feeling sick in the middle of watering and had to leave suddenly. I clean up around it before moving on to the other plants. This planter is one of my favorites. I found it at a flea market. It is made from pieces of stained wood arranged in a chevron design and on casters. I can easily bring it from the porch to the inside when needed. I have some of my peace lilies planted here and it was one of the first plants I bought when I moved in. I take the water and start tending to my other plants when my phone buzzes in my back pocket. It's from Darcy.

Hey. I just wanted to say sorry for acting like a jerk. I'm crabby from being sick and I shouldn't have taken it out on you. Forgive me? I'll buy dinner this coming weekend? We can all go out and celebrate the new year and Tim starting his new job this week.

I feel better after her apology and quickly text back letting her know all is forgiven. I can't wait to catch up with them. Tilting my head back considering something, I then send another text to Darcy.

Hey, I wanted to ask if you could go with me next week to my ultrasound? I know you aren't getting one. I'll be by myself. It might be nice to have someone there and you could get an idea on how both our babies are growing? It's next Thursday at 2pm. Let me know xoxo

Yeah, that would be great! Also, sorry I didn't get back to you sooner on those other texts. I dropped my phone last week and Tim just got my replacement this morning. I'll meet you at the hospital next Thursday. See ya then.

 Satisfied that everything is better between us, I finish up some chores, in the house, and relax for the rest of the day. I know I'll have a ton of work to catch up on, in the office, when I get back in tomorrow. With a baby on the way, I know peaceful afternoons like this are going to be few and far in between.

 A cold wind blows at my side, causing me to walk a little faster to the hospital for my ultrasound appointment. Darcy is already there waiting inside, by the front door. I'm so excited about today. I can't wait to see my baby moving around.

 As I walk inside the doors I call out to Darcy, "Hey! This is so cool. Thanks for coming out with me."

 We walk together, to the front desk, to get directions on where to go.

 She replies, "Of course, I wouldn't miss this chance to see the little one. I want to make sure everything goes well! Just as much as you do."

 Yeah, I can't quite pinpoint the way Darcy has been acting the past week. I've seen her shut down and go on auto pilot mode. I've seen her in just about every other emotion; but now, the way she has been acting, it is so strange to pinpoint. Almost like when someone is saying everything in a sarcastic way. Like a forced hospitality, but you know they don't really want to be nice. I asked Darcy if everything was okay, during our dinner last weekend.

 Darcy snapped at me, "Of course! Why wouldn't it be?"

 Even Tim looked up from his plate confused by her words and the hostility behind them. I've read, in an online article, that pregnancy hormones can make some women prone to bursts of anger and easily become irritated. I guess this is my life for the rest of our pregnancy. Twenty more weeks left. At least I get a break. Poor Tim has to live with her. I hope he doesn't end up dead by the end of this.

 Darcy has to wait in the lobby for the first part of the ultrasound. The ultrasound technician takes pictures and measurements for Dr. Lee. Noah and

I have decided not to find out the gender, so I let her know to keep it a secret from me. She moves the screen so I can't see while she checks out my baby's growth and normal development.

After about 10 minutes, she goes out to bring Darcy back in. We both stare, with awe, at the screen. We see the little shape move around in front of us. My cheeks hurt from smiling as I look at the little miracle in front of me. There is my baby. I can see its little toes and fingers. Oh, look! There is the spine!

I glance over at Darcy. She is leaning forward in her seat. Her eyes fixed on the screen as she rubs her hands over her belly.

She grips the side of the seat and asks, "What is the baby's sex?"

The ultrasound tech looks over at me as if I should respond.

"Oh, Noah and I aren't finding out until we deliver. We thought it would be more fun that way. I don't want to find out without him."

At this, Darcy frowns, "Oh, well I guess that should be fine."

Fine? What does that mean! It's not like she is finding out either. She won't even go in for an ultrasound or an exam. I'm not going to let her off the wall hormones ruin this special time for me.

I let my attention go back to the screen and treasure this time that I can look at my baby. I'm a little disappointed when it's time to leave. At least I got some cool pictures to take home. I can't wait to send them to Noah. Darcy asks for one and I pull out an image of a profile of the little face. A small part of me feels protective already, a pang of regret blooms because I gave away one small picture of my baby.

I feel like snapping at her to get her own, but I calm myself down by thinking I probably just need a snack. Darcy rushes off to get back to her schedule. I decide to take the rest of my day and walk around the mall, checking out some of the itty bitty baby clothes. My happiness is glowing around me. I can hardly feel the wind as it blows against me this time. Nothing is going to bring me down now. It can only get better.

Darcy

Hitting mute on the television, I can hear a car outside. It doesn't go past the house. I can hear it pull into the driveway. I know I'll have to see her eventually. I don't think my anger has subsided enough to be face-to-face, yet. Tim dropped off my new cell phone this morning, and there were two unopened text messages from Elena. I just deleted them, not even wanting to read them.

I sit still. Straining to hear what she is doing on her side of the house, I hear footsteps coming towards the door. Soon, I hear a knock at my door. Cursing under my breath, I steel myself for seeing her. I know I'll have to do this sooner or later – especially if my plan is to work.

Swinging open the door, I hold it with one hand and with the other I hold the door frame. Clearly indicating I want this to be quick. She looks surprised as she takes in my appearance. I can see she wants to reach out to me and I lean back.

"I've had a stomach bug for the past week. Tim and I actually canceled going home. I've been off work trying to recover. I must have gotten it from one of my patients. I'm slowly getting better. Don't worry."

I spit out the last words and try to remain calm inside. When I see her expression, she looks hurt. She seems to recover quickly as her face brightens.

"Well, okay. Let me know if you need anything. I hope this makes you feel better."

She shows me a small package wrapped with a big red bow, on the top. Still standing with the door open, I rip back the paper to reveal a small baby outfit. She says something about having the matching one but her words seem far away as I feel the anger start to rise up in me.

I force a smile and thank her before I close the door right in her face. I can't help it.

Walking over to the trash in the kitchen, I throw the romper and the wrapping paper in it. I take my hand and shove it down towards the bottom. Then, as an afterthought, I spit on it. That seems to make me feel better. I've acted like a fool in front of Elena. I need her to trust me. I take my phone and start typing up a text to apologize. It works. I knew it would. I know the real reason Elena is running from her past and trying to be so nice to everyone. She's not a pushover. She is just full of guilt. and that can sometimes be worse than being too trusting. She will do anything to make herself worthy, in others eyes. She needs my forgiveness, and of course, there is a certain price to pay. Lucky for her I take payments in blood.

Another ping goes off. This time Elena is asking me to go to her ultrasound. Ha! This is going to be so easy. I've taken advantage of the last couple of my days off to finalize my plan, in my head. The only part of my plan that could be traceable was ordering the prosthetic baby bump. If anything comes from that, I could just say I bought it as a gag for Tim to wear. You know, to show him how I feel with this big belly for a day. He would be so into it. He would look goofy and everyone would laugh at him. It's right up his alley. They really do sell anything online. I can't believe the number of people who ordered those things. It was a little expensive, but a small price to pay for a real baby. Now all I had to do was sit back and let Elena do all the work.

Going back to work last week was tiring. I think I've pretty much recovered now. The prosthetic belly came in the mail. I told Tim it was more maternity clothes when he carried the box into the bedroom, for me. I don't think I'll need it for a couple more weeks. I wear baggy sweatshirts and tuck some rolled up towels in the elastic waistband of my leggings. That seems to do the trick. One of the perks of it being winter is I can easily disguise things better. I also bought a large body pillow to use in bed. It takes up most of the space. There is no chance for Tim to get close to me. I tell him the last time we had sex, at the beginning of December, was very uncomfortable for me. We should probably wait until after the baby is born before doing 'it' again. I know he is annoyed about this news, but he doesn't say anything further. Even though I'm behind schedule, I make it a priority to go to the ultrasound with Elena. I want to know everything that is going on with this baby.

Getting into the hospital a couple minutes early, I can see Elena as she walks through the parking lot. The wind blows at her and she keeps her head down and walks faster. When she gets to the door, she smiles at me.

"Hey! This is so cool. Thanks for coming out with me."

Heading to the information desk together, I make sure I do my best to keep up the ruse and be level headed with her. I noticed I've been snappy with her lately. In order for this to work, I need to maintain some level of believability. Although, I could easily just blame this on hormones. I did have a cousin once who was a total monster her entire pregnancy. When she wasn't pregnant, she was the sweetest person you ever knew. She even once rammed into someone who had cut her off at the grocery store and blamed them for it!

Once we got situated, in the waiting room, the ultrasound technician took Elena back first to get some measurements and information for her charts. I wait and fiddle around on my phone. After about 10 minutes, the tech comes to get me. I'm feeling excited to get to see this baby. I know it's still in Elena, but I already feel like it's mine.

She turns the screen towards us and places the probe on Elena's belly. The screen jumps to life with movement. We both stare, in wonder, at the little body bouncing around. I can see the little fingers and toes and a little face. When my hands reach up to touch my belly, I'm reminded to keep them down and not lose focus.

"What is the baby's sex?"

I ask curiously because I want to start thinking of baby names, nursery themes and stuff I need to add to my registry. I'm forced to tell

Tim we can't have an ultrasound because I think it's too invasive and we won't be meeting with our midwife until the third trimester, to come up with a birth plan.

The tech looks at Elena and it's a reminder that I have no say in this decision. Elena looks at me and responds, "Oh, Noah and I aren't finding out until we deliver. We thought it would be more fun that way. I don't want to find out without him."

Just great. Okay, I can deal with that. I do feel a little sad because Noah will never actually learn the gender of his baby. By then, he will be long gone.

The technician prints off some pictures that were taken during the ultrasound. As we are leaving, I ask Elena for one. She seems to hold back a little and then gives me one of the pictures showing the profile of the face. It was just the one I wanted. Putting it away, I thank her and get back to my schedule. Having it in my pocket makes me feel better. This is a little piece of my baby I can carry with me everywhere.

Elena

My worries about the crazy hormone swings are pretty much gone with Darcy. She seems to be back to her normal self and is at ease around me again. With the long holiday weekend coming up, we both had a day off for Martin Luther King Jr. Day. We decided to drive to her parents house for the weekend. Tim is staying at home because he will not be able to get off work. It's strange to see him in dress slacks and a button up all the time. The old jokester is still there when he shows me what he got for the baby when we meet at the door on Saturday morning. A binky with a fake plastic mustache attached to the top. I tell him he will have to find one for me too!

The trip back to her parent's house takes about three hours. Halfway through, I ask Darcy if we can pull over somewhere to take a pee break. I don't know how she holds it in that long. My baby seems to love kicking my bladder. It's a wonder I don't pee my pants sometimes. I may not be showing that much, but still, I wasn't very big to begin with. I don't know how I'll manage when I get bigger. I'm currently in week 22, my baby is as big as a red bell pepper. According to my app, the baby should be almost one whole pound this week!

I love how rural her house is. It reminds me of the cabin we stayed at during our Labor Day getaway. It's crazy to think that was only a short time ago. So much has happened! There is a little bit more snow here than in Cincinnati. Darcy's father comes out to carry our bags and make sure we don't slip coming up the steps. Her mother is waiting inside and asks if we would like something to eat after the drive. She has some lasagna in the oven ready. I notice they dont hug when we get there, which is much different from Noah's family and when I greeted my grandmother when I was younger. Maybe this is why Darcy has such a reserved manner and usually avoids physical contact.

Regardless, my analysis of her family is disrupted by the delicious smell of the home cooked meal. Even Darcy can't wait to dig in. After our appetites have been satiated, it's time to get started on baby shower planning.

We have the invites laid out on the table and are going through some of the decorating ideas when Darcy's dad brings Tim's mother to the dining room, where we are working. I can see where Tim gets his high energy and friendly personality from. She goes around hugging everyone and has her own opinions on everything. By the end, Darcy and her mother seem to give up and let her do the planning. It's not that she is doing anything in a domineering, selfish attitude. Instead, it is more like she drank three cups of coffee and loves everything so much that Darcy and her mother can't keep up with her energy. They do whatever she suggests. I'm guessing it is to avoid any more hyper outbursts and to get her to stop talking. I love her! Her energy is a breath of fresh air.

We quickly get everything finalized and the invites complete. We have decided on a neutral woodland theme for the shower and our nurseries. The shower will be held at the family church and they already enlisted a group of women who would be making the food. All Darcy and I have to do is show up. Tim's father offered to use his truck to haul any big items back home for us. They said they would set them up too.

Filling out the baby registry, I don't feel comfortable asking for a lot of items from people I'm not familiar with. I end up putting some pretty basic items in my list. Darcy looks over at my list on my tablet and mentions I really don't need that much stuff starting off. Whatever I need, we can borrow from her stuff. That does seem to make sense, we will be having our babies together and be home during the same period of time. I imagine a blissful, slow summer holding my baby on the front porch while the hummingbirds dart back and forth from plants and the kids play in the street.

Waking up in the middle of the night, I was momentarily confused about where I was. I remembered I was sleeping in Darcy's little sister's old bedroom. I grab my cell phone and use it as a flashlight to find my way out in the hallway and to the bathroom. After I had finished and was heading back to my room, I heard a noise coming from the kitchen. It sounded like a door opening.

My heart started racing and I wasn't sure if I should wake anyone up. I tiptoed down the hall and slowly opened the door to Darcy's bedroom. The blankets were thrown back and the bed was empty. I felt relieved. The noise must have been Darcy downstairs. Curious, I walked quietly down the hall. While I crept down the steps, I looked towards the kitchen. Beyond the island was a little breakfast nook, with a small table and a couple chairs. Behind that was a sliding glass door where I could see Darcy sitting outside, on the porch, in the cold. What is going on? I walk over to make sure she is okay. She needs to get back inside. It's freezing tonight.

As I get closer, I can see her shoulders heaving up and down. I realize she is crying. I freeze. I know I should go to her and see what is wrong. Darcy is such a private person, I don't think she would like me to disturb her. She probably wouldn't tell me what's going on anyways. So I walk back to my room, as quietly as I can, and lay in bed wondering what could have possibly upset her so much. What ghosts of her past still linger in these halls? At least I would never have to go back to mine. The only place they could be found were in my distant memories and a small cardboard box.

The next morning Darcy's mother served us homemade waffles and strawberry syrup. Mmm… I could get used to this! I never was much of a cook.

As I'm savoring the last bite her mothers asks us, "Would you ladies like to accompany me to church today?"

Quickly, I looked at Darcy, hoping she would decline. I haven't been in a church in years. Just the thought of it freaked me out. A vision of walking in and God whispering in all their ears, telling them what I did pops into my head.

Thankfully, Darcy saved me, "Mom, I slept like crap last night, and honestly, I think we are going to head home after breakfast because we figured everything out yesterday. I have stuff I need to do tomorrow and I want to go to bed early tonight."

Her mother seemed disappointed but didn't let on, "Well, you certainly need your rest. Let me pack some snacks for the ride home and text me when you get there okay."

Darcy doesn't respond but just pokes at her waffles until they are a mushy clump. Then she gets up and throws them away. She starts to head upstairs to pack.

When I take my plate into the kitchen to rinse it off, I glance out the door and remember last night. There is nothing out there. It is just a small backyard that meets up with the woods. A storage shed sits in the back of the yard. That is probably where they keep a mower and garden stuff. A layer of snow covers everything else. Hmm… I guess this is another piece of the puzzle that is Darcy.

I see Jackie as I walk back into the office. I'm just about to tell her good morning, when my phone goes off.

"Hey, hold on, let me get this. It's probably Noah checking on how my appointment went today."

Fishing my phone out of my purse, I see Darcy calling. I step into the hallway for some privacy.

"Hey, I just got into work from my checkup. What's up?"

"Yeah, I remembered you had that appointment today. How did everything go? What did the doctor say about the ultrasound?"

I don't seem to remember Darcy being able to recall anything – unless she had it written down. I've had to tell her the types of plants in my house at least ten times. She has been able to remember my schedule pretty well lately.

"Yeah. Everything went well. He is happy with everything. Umm… I have to get back to work. We can catch up later or this weekend if you're not too busy."

"Oh, yeah. I have to go too. I just wanted to check in. When is your next appointment? Like a month?"

"Yeah. Next month. March 7th at 11am."

"Okay! Great! Talk to you later! Bye."

She hangs up before I get the chance to say anything else. I looked at my phone surprised. That was strange. Jackie is gathering up her stuff so we can switch places. I thank her before she leaves.

"Thanks for covering for me, Jackie. I'll put my next appointment in your schedule so you know when it is."

"Sounds good, Elena! It's no problem."

The phone, by my computer, starts ringing. As I start to get back into the rhythm of working, I feel grateful to work with such wonderful people. One of the other staff members even brings me little muffins and leaves them in the staff room fridge. I share a love of romance novels with an older woman who comes in on Fridays. She always leaves me her old books. I know Noah and I aren't sure if we want to move back to Nebraska or stay in this area, but I've come to love both and can't decide which I want more.

Pacing back and forth, in my living room, I am too excited to sit down. Noah should be arriving from the airport any minute now. I've spent the last several days cleaning the entire house. As soon as I got home today, I showered and shaved. We haven't seen each other since Christmas. It feels like it has been years. The only interaction we have is our selfies back and forth and our nightly phone calls. Sometimes, I feel like going to bed early. His daily update and wishing us a goodnight makes the lack of sleep worth it.

For Valentine's Day, Noah sent me a beautiful bouquet of roses. I have them sitting front and center on the coffee table. I check the water each day. A couple petals have fallen off, so I quickly scoop them up. I hear his rental pull into the driveway. I shove them into my back pocket. He will only be here for a couple days before he has to leave again. The hospital he is working at now offered him another contract. He agreed to take it with the condition he would be able to leave, without notice, to be with me when I go into labor. I probably won't see him again until I deliver the baby.

As he comes to the door and I rush out, onto the porch, to hug him. The door to Darcy's side of the duplex opens up, at the same time. Darcy and Tim come out to greet Noah. I'm feeling a little disappointed, I wanted alone time with him but I guess I can share him. Tim comes over and gives him a big hug even before I get the chance to.

He greets him, "Hey Man! Darcy said you were here and she thought it would be a great idea to take you out to eat tonight. I've been on a healthy diet with these two pregos. How about I share some wings and beer with you. My treat?"

Noah looks at me uncertainly. We had planned for a quiet dinner at home. I have some steaks in the fridge for later. I also got cupcakes from our favorite bakery around the corner. Even though I'm upset about the change in plans I know Tim and Noah will have fun. Noah and I will have later tonight to connect and all day tomorrow so I cheerily reassure Noah.

"Sure. Let's go out for dinner tonight, Noah. It will be fine."

The last thing I want to do is seem too needy or to make Tim think he was getting in the way. We all rode together. It seems to take forever to get our food. The place is packed with couples who had waited until the weekend for their date plans.

By the time we get home, I'm exhausted.

As we stand on the porch, Darcy yawns exaggeratedly, "Wow. I'm so tired."

She then rubs her belly for emphasis. Tim unlocks the door and ushers her in.

"Got to get the little one to bed. Goodnight guys. Hope we can see ya tomorrow for dinner."

As Noah and I get inside, Noah says, "It's been a long day, I bet you are tired, how about I give you a back rub and we relax."

I immediately feel deflated. I agree with him. When we lay in bed, I had hoped he would want to make love. When I try to kiss him, he cuts it short and whispers something about me needing to rest. Soon he is softly snoring in my ear.

I turn to my side as a tear escapes; rolling down my cheek onto the pillow. I'm so frustrated. Tonight was supposed to be just us. I had different plans that did not end up with me being tucked into bed. To make it even worse, Darcy made it a big deal about having a birthday dinner for Tim tomorrow night. His birthday isn't even for two more weeks. She wanted to make sure we were all together. We are going over there, at four tomorrow, to hang out. Maybe she doesn't care about special alone time with Tim because she sees him all the time. Is she that clueless? I want to spend an evening alone with my boyfriend because we hardly see each other.

I toss and turn that night. The next morning, I woke up irritable and tired. After we finished our breakfast and cleaned up, I was just about to mention that we should go downtown and check out some of the items from my baby wishlist. Noah's phone pings. It's Tim asking him to help assemble something for the baby. He promises it will not take long.

Another episode of some boring house renovation show starts, as Noah and Tim are still putting together items for the baby. For some reason, Darcy has bought a crib, bassinet and swing. She thinks now is the right time to assemble it because Noah is here for the weekend. He can help Tim, who seems to not even know what a screwdriver is for. To make matters worse they are both on at least their third beer.

Darcy calls out, from the kitchen, that she has ordered pizza for lunch. I'm starting to wonder if she is deliberately trying to sabotage my weekend.

"Hey Darcy, I was just wondering why you decided to buy all this stuff before our baby shower. I mean what if you get these things then?"

She acts surprised about the baby shower that we planned together!

"Oh, I guess I wasn't really thinking about that. I must be nesting or something. I've cleaned the house from top to bottom. I keep worrying about getting everything done because now that we are going to be in the third trimester… it just seems so real." Then she puts a hand to her mouth. "Oh my! Are we imposing on your weekend with Noah? I am so sorry. I am such an idiot."

She comes over to me and seems genuinely sorry.

"No, it's fine! Don't worry about it. We are glad to spend the weekend with you both. You are such good friends to us."

Noah has now stood up. Stretching out his back, from the awkward position of bending down to fit screws into the crib slots, he reassures them too.

"Hey, it's no big deal I'm just so thankful you are both here helping us out and watching over Elena while I'm away. It's been easier on me knowing she isn't alone."

So just like that, we spend the rest of the day there. Darcy puts on a movie, after dinner, and makes everyone ice cream sundaes. Tim is the first to fall asleep. His head back on the couch, jaw slack as he starts to snore.

Darcy elbows him awake and he sits up smiling, "Hey sorry guys."

He slurs, having spent the majority of dinner enjoying his present from Darcy: a thirty pack of beer. He graciously shared his present with his good pal, Noah, who is also buzzed.

I've had enough. I'm ready for bed. Forget the idea of sex. I just want to sleep. Standing up I ask Noah if he is ready.

"Yeah, I'm getting tired too. Let's head home."

The next morning I reach out my hand and the bedside is empty next to me. I look at the time on my phone and see it's past 9am. I know Noah had to leave for the airport by this time and I wonder where he is. He wouldn't leave without saying goodbye… would he? As I walk out to the kitchen, I see a note on the table. *Hey Beautiful, I didn't want to wake you because I know you need your rest. I'll text you when I get back to my room in Detroit. Love ya Noah.*

As I read the note again, a big, fat teardrop falls onto the corner, blurring the part where he wrote Love. For the first time in our whole relationship, a tiny sliver of doubt creeps into my mind. I silently wonder if this will work out.

Darcy

Being in the same room with Elena, and hiding my emotions from her, has finally become more manageable. I just keep reminding myself she will be dead soon so I won't have to worry about it much longer. Then, I'll have my baby and I'll be able to live the life I've always wanted. After the baby is a couple months old, I will convince Tim to get a vasectomy and I'll get on the pill again, just in case. I already know my uterus is cursed. I'll never be able to have my own baby.

When there are days I question what I am really planning on doing, all I have to do is redirect my thoughts to the images of my children. When I was a teenager, I knew that really wasn't my fault. The one person I shared my situation with was a careless doctor that didn't even give me proper medical treatment. She didn't give me options or support. I was just a dollar sign when I walked in. She didn't explain the procedure to me, and she definitely didn't let me know what would happen when she rushed me out of the office. Everytime I think back to that day I feel my chest tighten with anger and my breathing gets heavy like I'm walking uphill. *Here, take some ibuprofen for any cramping.* How about later on you are going to pass a small child from your body that we don't want to deal with and you can be emotionally scarred for the rest of your life. I'm not sure if that doctor did something to me when she was poking around in there, but I chose to blame her for not being able to carry my own child.

Then, there is Miss Perfect Elena, moving in with her *I love everyone attitude* and *I care about all things.* Waving to little babies in their strollers as we pass them, she is probably upset they were able to get past her claws. Well she is going to pay. So, yeah, I can deal with hanging around her now, because I envision her lifeless body instead of my childs when I look into her face.

When my mother first brought up the idea of a baby shower, I was excited about having a joint celebration with Elena. I had felt bad for her, not having any family nor close friends. Now, I'm going to my mothers for the weekend to make sure I invite everyone we know. I want her to see how much love and support I have. That's something she will never have.

Not only do I want to see her dead and childless, I want her broken emotionally too. I plan to go to my parents for the long holiday weekend and make it a big deal that Elena comes with me. I want her to be part of the planning and not feel left out. I want to keep up the appearance of best friends.

It's not until the morning we are packing and I'm having breakfast with Tim that I realize why I never go to my parents house in January. Ugh. I'll just have to shove down that memory and get through this weekend. I can do this, right? That was years ago and things are different now. I wonder if I can handle this though. I'm like a vase that was broken years ago, repaired and then dropped again; I'm breaking again along the old fractures. I'll have to be careful this weekend.

Pulling into my parents driveway, I find myself craving some alcohol. My old coping methods are starting to return. I'm not going to chance it. There is no way I'm going to ruin my end goal over a drink that someone catches me with or smells on me. I've got to stay sober.

After we get settled in and eat lunch, I busy myself with the assignment at hand: get everything planned and invites done for the baby shower. If I keep myself distracted all day, then I can get through this weekend without time left to worry. We are halfway through writing addresses on invites when Tim's mom comes into the room. I hold in my annoyance and smile when she pulls me in for a hug. When she goes to rub my belly, I think quickly reaching for her hand and redirecting it to my shoulder. I would never have to worry about that with my mom. We really aren't the touchy kind of family. Instead, opting for weird family photos where everyone has their arms around each other and we cringe for a couple shots saying cheese for the camera.

An hour later my mother and I have completely given away all control to Tim's mother. She is excitedly looking at everything with the same oohs and aahs as a child in Santa's workshop. It's easier this way. Her and Elena seem to be working much faster. We have everything done and we are just finishing up our registries by the time nightfall comes. I ask to look at Elenas to make sure we don't have duplicates.

When I take her stuff after she is gone, I don't want to have to return too much. She hardly has anything added to her list. It must be her guilt. That's fine, I'd rather have the baby shower and she walks away with nothing. After dinner, we watch a couple episodes of some stupid cooking show my mother likes then I excuse myself to go to bed.

After a couple hours scrolling through social media on my phone, I doze off. I'm soon caught up in a dream. I'm walking up the path to my front porch. Elena has her back to me. She is kneeling in front of a big planter on the porch with a cardboard box at her side. Her curly hair blowing in the breeze. I call out to her but she keeps working, spade in hand. She is taking dirt from the box and putting it in the planter. As I get closer and stand on the front step, I can see into the box. It's sagging at the corners, dirt and little human limbs poking out from the top as she takes another spadeful and starts humming as she continues working.

I call out to her again, in horror. I want her to stop, but she keeps transferring the gruesome soil mixture into her planter. Then, her arm goes out to the other side to grab a watering can. I'm frozen in place. I try to run as the red liquid housed within the watering can overflow from the planter. I can see it start running down the porch towards my feet. When I look up to scream at her again, Elena has turned to face me. It's not her face I'm looking into, it's my own.

I wake up inhaling sharply as if I was holding my breath. I fight for air as I sit up in bed. Throwing the covers off, I find the sheets are damp from my sweat. Standing up, I feel for my door and walk quietly out into the hallway and down the stairs. I find myself standing at the sliding glass door in the kitchen.

Going out on the porch, I slide the door shut behind me and lean back until my body braces against the cold glass. I slide down the door and I'm left sitting on the porch. The backyard is dark but the moonlight reflecting off the snow seems to illuminate everything. Ghostly shadows appearing from the trees and the shed. I put my head into my hands and sob. I stay out there until my feet throb and I think there is nothing left in me to cry. Then I sneak back upstairs and sit up in bed, on watch for the boogeyman. Scared like I was six years old again.

A notification for a scheduled reminder pops up on my phone. Oh yeah, today is Elena's checkup. I'm sitting with a patient going over some tips that she should be practicing, after a recent health issue. I tell her I have to call the office real quick, explaining there might be an emergency with another patient. Stepping into another room, I called Elena to check on how her appointment went. I don't want any surprises. If something would come up and she would need a certain medical care, I want to be well-prepared for any and everything. So far so good. Everything is going just as planned. She gives me the date of the next checkup and I put the information into my phone, so I don't forget. Going back into the room, my patient looks at me concerned.

"Is everything okay dear?"

I had almost forgotten my excuse to leave the room in the first place.

Smiling, I respond, "Oh yes, everything is great. I have a patient that is doing very well. I should even be discharging her from my care in a couple months. I just got a call with an update on her checkup."

This seems to make the woman happy. She sits back content. Oh yes... discharged, dead, what's the difference. At least I'll be putting her out of her suffering. I smile back at the lady, feeling pretty content too.

While Tim is getting ready in the bathroom, I sit on the bed drinking a smoothie and tell him how excited I am that Noah is coming home tonight. We should take him out to eat. I know it won't take much to get Tim excited, especially since we haven't gone out for the past month. I've purposefully told him how exhausted I've been and even faked a leg cramp so we would cancel our Valentine's plans. I know Tim will be excited to get out of the house. When I throw in beer and wings, he won't be able to resist.

After work, I stand by the front door, pretending to wipe the walls down when I see Noah's headlights pull into the driveway.

"Hey, Tim! Noah is here! Let's go out and say hi."

Without waiting for a response, I fling the door open. Elena's door opens at the same time. Tim is there next to me pulling Noah in for a hug.

Earlier, in the house, I urged Tim to wait for any snacks until we went out to eat. I know he is starving and he doesn't wait long to encourage Noah to go out for dinner. Noah looks over at Elena, as if asking for permission and she relents. I suggest a restaurant that I know will be packed and hope we have to wait for a table to prolong this night as much as I can. We get seats pretty quickly, but the waitress tells us one of the chefs called off, so they are short staffed and our food might take longer than expected. Of course, nobody wants to make the young girl upset because she already looks like she has had a rough night. We agree it's fine and we can wait. She smiles brightly and soon Noah and Tim are on their third beer. They are goofing off with each other.

Elena has been quiet and I can tell she is probably tired and hungry. I make sure to be excited and ask Noah all about his placement and plans for the next couple months. I excitedly proclaim that Noah and Elana should join us the next day to celebrate Tim's birthday too. I might have to work steadily the next couple weeks, so I made sure we were together this weekend. Yes, his birthday is in a couple weeks, but who cares. Between Tim and I, we occupy Noah's attention for the majority of dinner.

When we get back to the house, I make sure I yawn loudly. A clear reminder for Noah that being pregnant makes women very tired and he should probably let Elena sleep. I hope he feels bad about keeping her up and goes right to bed.

While Tim eats breakfast, I clean around him. I even make him move his feet so I can clean under his chair. When I'm done, there is another chore I have in mind. I know Tim will struggle with this one.

"Hey Tim, I'm feeling restless and I need you to put together those baby things I bought this week."

I give him a pouty face, for emphasis.

His eyebrows go up in surprise as he asks, "Darcy, you know I'm terrible at putting stuff together. Remember that stupid shelf I assembled and it fell apart nearly knocking me over. Do you really trust me to put something together that would be holding our baby?! Can't you wait until my dad comes after the baby shower."

Making sure I look defeated, I shrug my shoulders, "I guess, it's just that my hormones have been raging and I just want stuff ready. I guess I can wait." Then I brighten up, "Hey, I have a great idea! How about you call Noah to come over and help you! Please, it would mean so much to me!"

At this, I put my hand on his shoulder and he nods his head – warming up to the idea of getting more guy time. An added benefit and excuse to drink beer and goof off. He takes out his phone and calls Noah. Hanging up, he says they will be right over. This whole weekend is going even better than I thought it would. I'm thrilled with myself.

Dragging the boxes out of the hallway, Tim and Noah get started on the swing first. Noah soon finds that Tim has put his whole side together wrong and they have to tear it apart and start over. It's almost lunch by the time they are finished with that. They are just starting to work on my bassinet. I don't bother asking anyone when I call and order a pizza. When I shout out to them in the living room that lunch is on the way, I can tell Elena is starting to get annoyed.

She asks me pointedly, "Hey Darcy, I was just wondering why you decided to buy all this stuff before our baby shower. I mean, what if you get these things then?"

Looking up, I pretend to just now think about the shower, "Oh, I guess I wasn't really thinking about that. I must be nesting or something. I've cleaned the house from top to bottom. I keep worrying about getting everything done because now that we are going to be in the third trimester… it just seems so real." Putting my hands to my mouth I make my eyes go wide pretending to realize something important. "Oh my! Are we imposing on your weekend with Noah? I am so sorry. I am such an idiot."

This does the trick. When I rush over to Elena, she is already reassuring me that it's not a big deal. Noah is telling us how grateful he is to us too. Satisfied, I sit next to Elena and finish watching her show until the pizza comes. On the way to the kitchen, I trail behind everyone else and take some of the different sized screws Noah had set aside, in piles for the bassinet, and I casually reach down and mix some of them around. That should keep them busy for a little while longer. When Noah and Tim are finished with the baby items, Elena gets up to grab her phone charger from her place and Tim excuses himself to the bathroom. I seized this opportunity to talk to Noah.

"Hey, because we are alone, I had wanted to talk to you about Elena."

I have his attention instantly.

"Yeah, what's going on."

In a hushed voice, I continue, "Well, she has been venting to me about some stuff. I know you guys haven't been together long so I want to keep you updated. I want to make sure you both make it – especially with a baby on the way. Could I have your cell number and I'll text you later. I can use it in case something comes up and I need to reach you for an emergency."

He seems to be thinking about this and I know he is going through what could be annoying Elena in his head. He gives me his cell number. I hurriedly punch the number into my phone and slide my cell into my back pocket as Elena comes in the front door. He nods at me and I go to the kitchen to get started with dinner.

When Elena gives a friendly offer to see if I need help, I pull out the salad ingredients already prepared to keep her away from Noah. My gift for Tim, a 30 pack of beer, is a hit. He offers a new beer to Noah everytime he finishes his own. Soon, the guys are buzzed and Tim starts to fall asleep on the couch. Elena stands and makes it clear she is ready to leave. Noah follows after her. I can see he is a little unsteady on his feet. Perfect. After they leave, Tim falls asleep. I leave him alone on the couch. I'm ready for bed myself. This day has been very productive.

THE THIRD TRIMESTER

Elena

I was still feeling a little bit disappointed about the prior weekend with Noah. As I stand in my bathroom and look at my growing bump, I can't help but smile. I'm finally in my third trimester. I take a picture and send it to Noah. Week 28, big as a head of lettuce! I don't know when my stomach popped like this, but it seems everyday I'm feeling a little bigger. I'm getting to the point where I'm having trouble slipping on my shoes. I lost sight of my hoo ha weeks ago. It's time to go all natural and nobody will care about some hair on my bikini line when I'm giving birth.

Darcy has been extra attentive lately. She brings me part of her healthy dinners she makes and texts me daily to check up on how everything is going. I wonder if she is feeling apprehensive about her own progress and this is her way of feeling better. I would think it would be hard to not go to a doctor, for peace of mind, if nothing else. I guess home births have been around since the beginning of time. With Darcy being a nurse she would be able to take better care of things than I would. She must have a high pain tolerance to go through that naturally. Not me, I prefer to be sedated and not feel anything when this baby comes. I have a low pain tolerance. I hope they numb me up real good.

If I was feeling optimistic at the beginning of the month, my life has taken a turn for the worse. I should have known. Maybe by keeping that box as a reminder, to strive to do better, has actually let evil into my life. The contents slowly leaking out like carbon monoxide. I couldn't see or smell the poison, but it was killing everything that was once a source of life and joy for me. Over the month of March things just got worse and worse. First it was with Noah. Our conversations got fewer and fewer. He kept making excuses on why he couldn't call. I wasn't going to push the issue because I thought he was just busy and tired after working so hard. Doubts about his infidelity started to creep into my thoughts. Last night, I tried to call him about my week. We had a huge argument, on the phone, and we aren't even talking now! I was so upset I called off work the next day. Not that they would care. That's another thing, it seems like everyone at work has been avoiding me. They've suddenly developed an icy shoulder towards me. When I walk into a room, they stop talking. There are no more gifts in the fridge and the one therapist asked if I still had any of her books because she would be needing them back. The only consistent I've had has been Darcy. She is always there when I need to talk and has been so protective over me.

My body has also turned on me. I'm becoming so big I can hardly find a comfortable position at night. When I do get comfortable, I have to get back up to go pee. My lower back is always strained. Sometimes, just for good measure, my baby gives me a good, sharp kick right to my ribs. My skin stretched tight over my belly and it itches constantly. Sometimes, at night, when I know I shouldn't, I scratch it gently. I swear, it's almost like an orgasm. Even though it leaves my skin red and inflamed. I just lather it back up again with lotion hoping to satisfy it until the next time. Then there are the hot flashes. Once, at work, I went to the bathroom and took off my clothes in the stall to try and find some relief. I was glad April was here so I could start opening my window and getting some fresh spring air to cool me off.

Darcy hasn't seemed to be having any issues with her pregnancy. She has started wearing cute maternity clothes and ditched the oversized sweaters. Her perfect little bump is adorable. She walks with ease while I'm left waddling beside her. While we were out to eat last night, I asked her how her meeting with the midwife went.

She casually responded, "Oh. I'm not really worried about it. I went with whatever she suggested. I told Tim to take notes and get everything we would need for the house."

I find that bizarre. With how Darcy is a control freak, I can't believe she would leave this all to Tim! I mean, come on. I love him, but I wouldn't trust him to be prepared to remember everything I would need for my home birth! At least I'm glad they are working together so well.

I've already confirmed with Darcy that I will call as soon as anything happens. She will stop whatever she is doing and take me to the hospital. She plans to be there for the delivery too. I was curious about the plan if I delivered at the same time as her and she just brushed off my concern. She said the chances were very rare that it would happen, and that she would be there for me. I don't know if Noah wants to come. The last time we spoke, he told me he needed space. I'm waiting for him to make the next move.

The scenery flies past my window in a blur. I don't seem to focus on anything. April is the perfect month for my mood. Rainy days matching my feelings and inviting me to wallow in self-pity for as long as I wish. Darcy and I are heading back from the joint baby shower. The whole thing was so miserable. I felt like such an outsider. Darcy was the star of the show. There were so many people there and they all knew each other. Darcy seemed caught up with everything. I was mostly left alone or finding myself trying to help with cleaning up. I tried to stay out of the way. There were a couple people who bought me gifts and the occasional box of diapers. I'm not complaining at all. It was almost harder to pretend I was interested when I knew I wouldn't be able to share any of this with Noah.

When we get back, Tim carries my stuff in and sets it on the couch. He then leaves to help his father who has followed us in his truck to haul Darcy's bounty. She ended up getting a swing and bassinet just like I thought. She already told me she is just going to return them and get money for something else. A part of me was hurt. She didn't offer to give them to me. I try to brush off that thought; I don't want to be selfish. She has already done so much for me. She has regularly taken off time to drive me to appointments. I told her she didn't have to, but when I was at work last week she texted me that she was outside the building and ready to take me to my 33 week checkup. Pretty soon, I'll be going weekly. I wish I could do something to slow it down. I remember how I used to be so happy about this baby. Maybe when the baby comes, I'll feel differently.

Darcy

Growing up, I wasn't really into games. Rather, I preferred to read alone for most of my time. My brother taught me the game of checkers. He beat me on so many occasions that when I did win, I wasn't sure if I beat him because I was good or he intentionally lost. It's bothered me ever since. This time though, I know I'm winning. Just like in checkers, I've double-checked each move and I've trapped my opponent into a corner. I've taken out her defenses and left her with no option other than to submit to me. By the end of March, I get compliments on my "pregnancy glow". I know it's just my sheer happiness shining through.

The first person I knew I needed to get rid of was Noah. That was surprisingly easier than I thought it would be. They weren't the love-sick destined soulmates they let on to be. After I had Noah's cell phone number, I made sure to start putting the first cracks in their foundation. Debating between texting him or calling him, I decided it would be better to call. I didn't want him to send screenshots to Elena. The whole plan could backfire. So, the week after he left, I called him.

He picked up on the first ring, "Hey, It's Darcy. I just wanted to touch base and give you a heads up about some of the things Elena has been upset about. You know, so you can hopefully avoid any conflict. She is probably worried about telling you because you guys don't see each other often. Long-distance relationships can be hard."

I hear him moving on the other side of the line. He shut a door behind him, probably to get some privacy. I know Elena has said he is sharing a house with three other roommates.

After some more shuffling he replies, "Hey, thanks for calling. Yeah, what's been bothering her?"

"She has been very tired lately. She doesn't know how to tell you. It's hard on her when you call every night and keep her up. I'm not sure what to do about that because I know your schedules conflict. Maybe text her or give her a call on her lunch break or something?"

He seems to be thinking about this information, "I guess I never thought about my calls being too late. I could call her on her lunch break. It's tough though. I know sometimes she eats at her desk and there are people in the waiting room. Has she said anything else?"

I take a pause and then answer him. "Hmm... nothing I can think of right now. Please don't say I told you anything. I'm trying to help you guys out. Elena is such a good friend to me. If there is anything else, I'll call you. Take care Noah, goodbye!"

"I appreciate it, Darcy. You take care of yourself and the baby, too. Thanks and I won't say anything. Bye."

At the end of the week, when I bring over some chicken salad for Elena she seems quiet.

Hoping my plan has been working, I ask her, "Hey, is everything okay?"

She rubs her neck as she answers me, "It's Noah. You know how we usually do our nightly phone calls? Well, he has stopped calling me at night. We only got to talk a couple times this week, when I was able to have someone cover for me at the front desk. He seems distant or something. He keeps asking me if it's okay to talk, as if it's too much of a bother to talk to me."

I sit down across from her.

With a concerned look on my face, I respond, "Hmm... that's so strange, hmm..."

I don't finish my sentence but instead act like I'm holding something back and Elena takes the bait.

"What is it? What are you thinking?"

"I shouldn't say anything. It's probably nothing. I do remember one of the other home nurses talking about Noah being very flirtatious in the office. I just ignored them because he is very friendly. That was very early on in your relationship, when he lived here. It was not as serious as it is now for you guys. I'm sure he is just very busy working all those hours."

Now Elena is holding her neck and rubbing her forehead with her other hand. She appears more stressed than when I came in. She doesn't say anything. I can see her working over the possibility of Noah's infidelity in her head.

I take that time to leave, "I should have never said anything Elena! Don't worry about it. Guys don't talk as much as women. He is probably tired from working and living with those guys. They probably drink beer and watch sports during their time off. I have to get back and get ready for work tomorrow. Talk to you soon, okay!"

I shut the door behind me quietly and leave her to own thoughts. I know sometimes that can be the worst. When you are left alone with your insecurities and doubts.

Creating a stressful work environment was next on my list. When I pull up to Elena's office, I text her that I'm there to take her to her 33 week checkup. I wait until she is in the car before I launch the next attack on her allies. Since I came early I told her to wait and I'd be right back. I made up a story about needing to see if I can get a referral started for one of my clients that has been depressed. When I walk into the outpatient clinic, I see the woman, Jackie, who covers while Elena is gone. I'm dressed in my hospital scrubs. I feel like that already gives me a level of trust in the office. I come up to the window and look around as if I'm about to give a big secret. I can tell I have Jackie's full attention.

"Hey, I was just here to pick up my neighbor, Elena, for her appointment. I was actually the one who helped her get this job."

At this information, Jackie relaxes a little, realizing this is a friendly conversation. I'm not there to inquire about my own outpatient therapy.

She replies, "Oh, yes! We love having her around the office. Thanks for the recommendation."

I glance around the room again acting nervous as I speak in hushed tones, "Don't say I told you. I feel guilty because I was the one that referred Elena. I don't want your office to be left hanging. Elena told me she plans on quitting right before the baby comes. She didn't want to let you guys know because she thought it would ruin her chances of you guys throwing her a surprise shower or getting her gifts. She was going to leave about a week before she was due. She really says the most awful things about working here!"

I can tell the woman is shocked by this news. I try to look sympathetic.

"I have to go. Elena is waiting in the car. She asked me to pick her up because she hates driving herself. Not that my schedule matters. Whatever. I'm trying to be a good friend."

As I turn to leave, I see another therapist walking into the little front office space. They both start talking in whispers. The lady at the front desk now has a scowl in place of the smile from a couple minutes ago.

That night when Elena got home, I invited her over to visit. I anxiously waited to hear about the rest of her day. I sat across from her, on the couch, impatiently tapping my foot until she finally got her shoes off. It was so annoying watching her struggle with her sneakers. When is she going to switch to slip ons?

When she is finally sitting I ask, "So, how did the rest of your day go? Anything exciting at the office?"

She sat back and blew up her cheeks and slowly let the air out, "I don't know what happened. When I came back, it was like everyone was acting differently. Jackie was at the front desk. when I walked in, she grabbed her stuff and went down the hall without saying anything. Nobody came out of their offices. Then when they left for the day, everyone just walked past me without even glancing in my direction. I'm not sure if it was something I said or if they are just mad I'll be taking time off for my appointments and maternity leave. I messaged Jackie and asked her if there was anything wrong and she responded that everyone is super busy and had lots to take care of. I shouldn't worry."

I give her my full attention. I'm acting as if I'm listening with concern but inside I'm doing somersaults.

"That is so weird. They are probably annoyed that they have to do something for themselves for once. I know you do way too much there. Sounds like you work with a bunch of selfish losers. Don't even worry about them."

She seems to consider this as she twirls a piece of hair between two fingers.

"Yeah, I guess you're right."

As we are sitting on the couch, I reach up and pull off Tim's hoodie. Revealing my "new" baby bump under a tight shirt.

She immediately notices, "Oh my gosh, Darcy! Look at your bump! You've kept it hidden under all those sweaters. It's gotten so big."

Last night, I started wearing my prosthetic baby belly. I've decided since it's getting warmer, I won't be able to get away with the baggy hoodies anymore. I'm just going to wear it all day long so I'm used to it. I'll only take it off for showers from this point on.

With all the progress I made in March, I decide I can move forward with my ballsier plans this week. Emboldened by my earlier successes, the first thing I did was reach out to an old colleague from the home nursing agency. There was a nurse named Nikole that used to work for us. I had met her a couple times. It's not like we were close friends, but we had worked for the same patient and shared thoughts on their progress.

I still had her cell number. After she quit and went to work in the hospital, there were rumors going around the office that she was under investigation for missing medications. Because there was no way to prove it, the office couldn't do anything about it.

I sent her a text asking if we could meet up that afternoon because I needed help. She didn't ask what was wrong but just sent back a time and place. As if she already knew what kind of help I needed.

An hour later, I was pulling up to the hospital. I found the picnic table she had told me about. I took out my brown paper bag from the fast food restaurant I stopped at on the way and sat down to wait.

About fifteen minutes later I saw her walking over, "Hey Darcy, so what's going on?"

Instead of sitting, she chose to stand next to me. Like she was about to leave if this conversation wasn't worth her time or if she didn't feel comfortable. Cautious. Like she didn't trust my intentions.

"Hey, I know this is weird, me getting in touch with you out of nowhere. I need help with something. I'm dead set on having a home birth but my husband already told me he is taking me to the hospital if anything goes wrong or if labor is taking too long. I was thinking I could speed up the process, on my own, at home, if I used some pitocin. It would cause my contractions to come consistently and I could administer it myself safely. He wouldn't even know. Then we could all get what we wanted."

She stood there, not saying anything. I handed her the brown paper bag and she looked inside and saw the bundle of hundred dollar bills at the bottom.

"It's a ten-piece meal," I said, referring to the money at the bottom.

I had hoped a grand would be persuasive enough. Now she closed the bag and held on to it.

"Meet me here next Wednesday, same time and place."

At that, she turned and walked back inside. As I got back into the car, my hands were shaking when I placed them on the steering wheel. The whole thing went smoothly, for a drug deal. I knew for my plan to work, I would need the pitocin to give to Elena so her contractions would speed up and I could force her to deliver the same day I took her. I really needed Nikole to come through for me. There was no way I could get pitocin from my office. We didn't work maternity care and I didn't have access to medications in a hospital without using my badge and code. I certainly didn't want to be caught snooping around the maternity section inside the hospital. I was already in too deep. I decided to make my next move before I lost the courage. I called Noah. Again, he picked up quickly. He must carry his phone with him all the time. Constantly worrying about his precious little Elena. Well, now it was time to shatter that image.

"Hey Noah, I've been putting off calling you. I just feel so bad. I know what a good person you are and you deserve to know the truth." The other end of the line is quiet, but I can tell he is still on so I continue. "Elena told me this week that she isn't one-hundred percent sure the baby is yours. She had been seeing someone on-and-off that she knew from Texas. They saw each other around the same time you guys hooked up. With her being a little smaller than I am, in the belly, she was thinking she might not be as far along as she thought. That guy has been calling her lately and Elena thinks she might have the baby and not tell anyone. If the baby looks like you, she will tell you it's yours. If it looks like this other guy, then she will tell him it's his. I'm so sorry to tell you this news. You deserve to know. Please don't say I told anything! You should ask her about her past and what she used to do. Hasn't she shared any of that with you?"

I'm betting on the fact that Elena is so tight lipped about her past that she also wouldn't have shared it with Noah. My suspicions are confirmed when he lets out a deep breath. I'm wondering if he is crying.

"No, she hasn't told me anything. She just says there is something from her past she isn't ready to share. I haven't pressed her about it. Now that you say something, it makes me think about this time I almost opened a box under her bed. She just about freaked. It was probably full of stuff from that other guy. How could I be so stupid!"

"I'm so sorry, Noah. Maybe, if she calls you after the baby is born, and does tell you it's yours, you could suggest getting a paternity test. You could ask her later about her past and see if she opens up about this guy. What if they are even married and thinking about getting back together. I don't know. I do remember seeing a paper at her house with a different name, so that would explain it."

I try not to smile because I want to seem very serious, even though I'm on the phone. It seems to be working because Noah is very quiet.

It's even the truth. I did find a different name. I know if he mentions it to Elena and she gets defensive and denies it, he will know she is lying. He will assume it's because she is married and doesn't know if the baby is his. I'm hoping by feeding him these lies and stoking the fires of his possible playboy behavior with her that when they do talk their tempers will be too hot to have a civilized conversation. Now I just wait.

I have the afternoon off to meet up with the midwife at the house, so I take some time organizing before she comes. Tim arrives just a couple minutes before her. I instruct him to take the notes for our meeting and tell him he is in charge of getting everything she wants us to have. His jaw drops in surprise. I don't think he can believe that I would trust him with this task. Not that I care what he does or forgets. It won't matter. I'm not going to worry about running around collecting things for some bogus home delivery when I already have one to plan with Elena. I can't wait for the meeting to be done as I sit pretending to listen to her explain the steps for our home delivery. She went over all the possible outcomes as Tim pays enough attention for the both of us. He scrawls notes down and makes a list of what she suggests we have on hand. I almost feel bad for him because he looks so frazzled by all the information.

After she finally leaves, I act so grateful and let her know we will continue to keep her updated and will be in touch with any issues that might come up. Texting Elena, I'm curious if she has talked to Noah yet. Her cheery response about meeting for dinner tells me otherwise. I had hoped we could talk about the failings of her relationship over dinner. Now I'm stuck making small talk about work and her pregnancy symptoms.

During our dinner that evening, I eat fast and find myself tapping my fingers on the table until she takes the hint and asks for the check and a to go bag. Later that night, as I'm watching some stupid action movie with Tim, Elena calls me crying. She had a bad fight with Noah and needs me to come over. Rushing to get up, I knock over Tims drink. I don't even care. I leave it for him to clean up, even though I know he will leave a mess for me to handle later. He is so unthoughtful, like that. I guess it is why I have to take care of anything I want done correctly.

When I get into Elena's house, I find her sobbing on the bed. There is a pile of toilet paper in her hand that she is using to wipe at her nose. Her phone is laying at her side.

"What happened? What did you guys fight about?"

I sat next to her on the bed anxiously waiting to hear.

"I don't know. I called him because I missed him and he was so short with me. He said he didn't have time to talk and something about maybe there was someone else I should be calling. Acting like I was the one cheating. I asked him if I should be asking him the same thing and then he sort of exploded. He accused me of not being upfront with him and hiding something from my past. I told him there were things from my past that I wanted to share with him, but that I didn't want to do it over the phone. He just told me to save it and said that it might be best if we had some space. He told me to call him after the baby was born and we could talk then!"

At this, she starts sobbing again. She is making annoying noises and I know I should comfort her. I don't want her tears or snot on me, so I just rub her leg in support.

"I always felt he wasn't good enough for you, Elena. I'm so sorry that happened. Maybe this is a good thing. Tim and I are here for you and don't you forget that. Don't even try to call him back. Someone who acts like that doesn't deserve you."

She nods her head slowly and I ask her if she needs me to stay with her. She grabs some more toilet paper from the roll she has on the bedside table.

"No, it's okay. Thanks for coming over and listening to my stupid problems."

As I look into her red, teary-eyed face, I reply, "Sure. It's no problem. Friends 'til the end, right?"

As I leave for work the next day, I see Elena's car is still in the driveway. I go to her door and start knocking. Soon she swings it open. Her eyes are red and puffy. Her face is mottled from crying all night.

I ask, "Hey, I was just checking on you. No work today? Are you doing alright?"

She leans against the door frame, "I called off. I didn't sleep last night and I just wanted to be alone today."

"Call me if you need anything, alright? Try to get some rest. We have the baby shower this weekend. I know that will cheer you up and give you a distraction from all this Noah crap."

As I turn to go to my car, I look back and yell over my shoulder, "I won't take no for an answer. This baby shower will be good for you, Elena. Okay? I'll bring you home dinner tonight and talk to you then."

Elena waves from her door as I pull out. Usually the rainy weather in April gets me down. This month, when it starts to sprinkle on the way to my first patient's house, I turn on some cheery pop music and sing along loudly in my car; thumping my hand on the steering wheel. I know there is going to be a rainbow at the end of my storm.

Opening another present, I'm surprised at how excited I've been today. On any other occasion, I would have been mortified. Today is different, because this is my baby shower. It is the culmination of all the hard work I've put in over the years. I've enjoyed being around all my family and friends. They've made me the center of attention. Presents are coming from all angles. I've finally earned the chance to take it easy on myself. Things have never been better. My mother and I have patched up our relationship. Tim has a commendable job. All my colleagues and patients look up to me and respect me. And best of all, I don't have to go through the pain of a full-term delivery. Elena is doing that for me. All my meticulous planning has paid off. Once she delivers, I'll call it even for the revenge I want to exact on the people of my past.

Elena stands for everything that went wrong a long time ago. Today, I don't even want to spend any time thinking about her. The best part is, I have her right where I want her. She depends on me. I'm the only person in her life right now. With a baby on the way, I know even if I act like a total jerk, she will still need me. I spend the day talking with my friends and family. Ignoring Elena is easy. I make sure I have my mother and Tim's mother sit at my table. I accidentally forgot to leave a spot for Elena.

When I spot her, she is sitting in the back of the room absentmindedly looking at her phone. I bet she is hoping for Noah to text or call her. I smile and sit back enjoying another bite of cake. There are only a couple boxes of items that fit neatly in my back seat that are for Elena. The rest of the things are for me. Tim's father follows us home. He said he would haul the items that didn't fit in my vehicle and he would help set them up.

Elena is quiet on the way home. Constantly looking out the window spacing out. That's fine with me, I don't have anything to say to her. When we get back, I make it a point to have Tim and his father leave the bassinet and swing by the door, mentioning to Elena it's so I can return them for money. She probably thought I was going to offer them to her. I wanted the satisfaction of her asking, which she doesnt do. The stress of money while she is off work and then the cost of childcare is probably weighing heavily on her mind. Poor little Elena, what a mess you've gotten yourself into.

Elena

Getting out of the shower, I dry off and do the ceremonious rubbing of oil on my belly. As I'm almost done getting dressed, I catch sight of myself in the mirror. Today is Monday. The day I would usually take a selfie of my bump and chart my weekly progress. Despondently, I hold up my phone but I can't find the reason to care anymore. I put it back down as I continue to dress. I blink to hold back the tears. Staring back at myself, in the mirror, I wonder if I have the strength to go through with this. A voice in the back of my mind encourages me that I am strong. I was made and raised with tremendous love. As long as I cling to that, everything will be fine.

The trick might just be to convince myself of this because it feels like a rain cloud hovers over my life. Today is the start of week 36. My baby is as big as a honeydew melon. The weight of my belly is nothing compared to the weight I feel on my shoulders. I feel as if it weighs me down with each step. Last night, when I finally found a comfortable position – a pillow propped under my belly and one between my knees – it was my mind that couldn't find peace. Thoughts of Noah and my dwindling finances bouncing around until I finally fell into a troubled sleep.

Instead of going to the kitchen to start preparing lunch for work, I find myself standing in the closet staring at the pile of beach towels in the corner. Without really thinking about it, I pull them down and throw them onto the floor. Today I will confront my demons. I pull down the box with the words 'special stuff' scrawled on the side, in marker. I take it to the living room and set it on the couch beside me.

Hesitantly, I lift the lid up just enough to pull out the first item. It's a wooden plaque from the women's health clinic I used to work for. My name in bold golden letters with the words, *In appreciation to one of our most valued workers, you make a difference in people's lives everyday.* At one time, I used to be so proud of this plaque. It was displayed over my head everyday at work. I managed the funds for our office and participated in fundraisers for abortions our clinic provided for those who couldnt afford it. It wasn't until later that I actually realized our clinic was certainly making a difference in lives. We were ending them. I was so adamant about abortion being a womans right and a freedom. It was essential for our equality and liberation from society. Without it, we would be slaves to our ovaries. I forgot who it really hurt the most, the same people I advocated for and marched for, women.

I placed the plaque down and reached into the box. The next item was much smaller. the words on it written in lead instead of gold. Each letter is one hundred times more valuable and heavy on my heart. It was the suicide letter from my previous roommate. I swallow back the dread rising in my throat and read it again.

> Maria,
>
> I'm so sorry you had to be the one to find me like this. But I wanted there to be one person I could share my story with. Someone that would protect it. Please don't tell my family. I can't bear for my mother to find out what I did. Them wondering why I did this is better than them knowing the truth. If they say anything, just tell them all you know is I loved them very much and it's not their fault.
>
> There are things you hide away from everyone but you can never truly hide it from yourself. It follows you and torments you. It wears you down. Last year, before we became roommates, you already knew I was in a relationship that ended badly. But, what you don't know is, I was pregnant. I did what anybody would do when forced into a tight spot with a man who runs off with another woman. I did the thing everyone I knew told me was my right. It would make everything better. I had an abortion. But that's not the worst part. The worst part is I drove to New Jersey where the doctor would see me because I was almost 9

months pregnant. At the time, I thought of this as my right as a woman and to be honest my revenge on my ex. I was so selfish then and I thought it was no big deal. Shortly after it was done, I was drawn in by some video from pro lifers on my social media feed. I was just about to leave a comeback to someone's comment when the next image on the screen showed a baby. The baby wasn't one of those pictures you see wrapped up in a blanket smiling at the camera. It was dead, laying on a medical tray as if it were a tumor someone had cut out and could now dispose of with the other bloody rags. Instead of leaving the comment, I found myself reading the article and the truth hit me so hard on what I had really done that I could hardly recognize myself in the mirror anymore. I felt the darkness start to swallow me and the burden I was carrying was almost too much to bear. At times, it almost seems I can still feel my baby moving inside of me, like a phantom limb.

I marched in the protests. I wore the rainbows. All the while, I was busy growing my instagram and living with such anger everyday at all these social injustices. I woke up one morning and realized the world didn't even notice I was lost. All the yelling and screaming and nobody even heard me. It had been months since I spoke to my mother and I was too busy to attend anything at my family's holiday functions because I thought I was above all the archaic traditions. I hurt the only person who never did anything wrong to me and just wanted a chance to live. I was no better than the very people I fought against every day. The darkness seeped into my thoughts until it felt like it was oozing out of my every pore. I can't live like this anymore. I can't go on because I don't deserve a good life. Please understand this so you don't ever get sucked into the path I went down and you can change what you are doing and what that place you work for does everyday.

Liz

Now the tears come. I don't try to hold them back anymore. I pull the letter to my chest as I rock back and forth. The memory as fresh to me as if it was branded to my brain. There was a work function I had attended late that night. When I got home, I heard music coming from the bathroom.

Everything else in the apartment was quiet. All the lights were off. Flipping on the hallway light, I called out to Liz. There was no answer. I tried calling her cell and I heard the music in the bathroom stop. A phone started buzzing. The buzzing continued until the phone fell onto the floor with a loud thud. Slowly, I walked down the hall. I was too afraid to say anything. A part of me already thinking the worst.

Over the past month, I had seen Liz draw into herself more and more. One night, when we watched a movie, she commented on how she thought death would feel. It was such a strange moment. I playfully hit her with a pillow and told her to stop being so dramatic. My life was too busy and there was no time to focus on anyone but myself.

When I flipped the light switch, in the bathroom, I saw Liz laying in the tub. The red water was thick around her body. It was just as still as she was. I didn't scream out. Instead, choosing to pretend there was still time. I pulled Liz up from the water. I dragged her body over the side of the tub as the red water spilled out around us. She fell into my lap and I tried to slap her face. I called her name, but nothing happened. I could see the cuts on her wrist. I closed my eyes and buried my face into her hair. Through tears, I called 911 to save her but I was too hysterical on the phone. I had to run next door and get a neighbor to help.

It wasn't until later that night, after the police had left, that I found the letter. She had left it under my tablet, where it would be hidden from sight. That same night, I packed up my stuff, emptied my bank accounts and decided on a fresh start. It was the best way I could cope at the time.

Putting the letter aside, I reach into the box for the last item. A framed picture of my grandmother holding me when I was a toddler. She is sitting on a white rocker and smiling proudly at the camera.

As I rub a finger across the glass, I ask out loud, "Please grandmother, tell me what to do?"

A memory comes to mind. I was in middle school and came home in a bad mood. Throwing my backpack on the floor, I stomped into the kitchen giving my best sassy teenager attitude to my grandmother.

She raised her eyebrows at my behavior, I looked right at her and said, "Yeah, what are you looking at?"

Instead of saying anything, my grandmother surprised me by grabbing her car keys and telling me to follow her. Confused on why I didn't get a lecture on respect, and also feeling a little guilty about how I acted, I did as I was told. When we got to the park, I was now feeling ashamed. I was ready to apologize when she directed me to a bench in the shade of a big oak tree.

"Grandmother, I'm sorry. I don't understand why you took me to the park. I'm a little too old to play here anymore. I really don't deserve it for taking out my anger on you."

A smile played at the corner of my grandmother's face as she whispered to me, "Let me tell you a little secret. I don't take you to the park for you. It's for me."

Puzzled by what that meant, I furled my eyebrows and tilted my head at her.

At this, she laughed and explained, "You see, everytime I think I've had enough or when you were little and were going through an active day, this is where we always came. You ran around until all your energy was out. It renewed me seeing you so happy and full of life. After you got older and I was missing your mother or going through something of my own, I would come here and watch all the people. I would forget my own sorrows. See, look at that little girl on the swing. See how big her smile is. Now look at her mother. Right now, she is forgetting about the tantrums and sleepless nights. All she sees is her beautiful child and the reason why it's all worth it. There is nothing you are going through that a child's laughter won't heal."

At the time, I thought my grandmother was being ridiculous. Now, I find myself slipping on some sandals. I put everything back into the box and place it on the top shelf of the closet. I don't even care about calling off work. I leave my phone on the table. Today, I'm going to the park.

There couldn't be a more beautiful spring day. It seems everyone is taking advantage of it. I find a bench near the playground and start to feel better as I focus on the smiles and laughter around me. I realize this is what my grandmother was talking about. For the first time in weeks, I saw a small glimmer of light at the end of my tunnel. My baby must feel it too, because at the same moment, I feel it push up against my skin and I reach down. We touch. I'm just wondering if I'm feeling a little hand or foot when a young woman almost falls over my outstretched legs.

Shocked, I asked her, "Oh my! I'm so sorry, are you okay?!"

Reaching out to see if she is okay, she bends over and rubs her ankle.

"It's not your fault. I wasn't paying attention. I do think I rolled my ankle a bit. Do you mind if I sit here for a minute?"

Moving my purse to the other side, I make room for her.

"Yes. Please sit down. Again, I'm so sorry. Do you want me to go get you some ice?"

The woman smiles at me and I feel a hint of recognition. Maybe she was the lady at the pharmacy, or the bank?

"No. Don't worry about it. I'm sure it will be fine soon. I came here to think anyway. There is someone I'm worried about and I thought I could think about how I could help if I came here."

"Oh, I came for the same reason. I have some things on my mind I was hoping to find clarity on." I need to help myself.

"Maybe I can help. I think I'm very good at giving advice."

She smiles at me brightly and for some reason I feel I can trust her. I hesitate. I'm just about to say it's no big deal and change the subject on my delivery fears, when another memory from my grandmother pops into my thoughts. This time from when I was about seven.

I had been playing on the back deck when a splinter went deep into my palm. Afraid my grandmother would take her needle and make me sit while she dug it out. I choose to keep it hidden from her. For about a week, I made sure to avoid bumping it and did my best to keep it out of her sight. Before I knew it, the spot was red and swollen. One day, when washing up for dinner, my grandmother came up behind me. She was waiting to use the sink when she noticed I was washing my hands strangely. Narrowing her eyes she grabbed my wrist and turned my hand so my palm was facing her. There was no avoiding this so I just let my head drop in defeat as she led me to the table and pulled down her first aid kit.

"Maria, you can not let an infection get this bad. If you have something like this, please let me know so I can help you."

In a tiny voice, I responded, "Sorry, grandmother. I had a splinter and I was afraid of the needle."

My grandmother seemed to consider this.

She spoke again in a softer voice, "I know you may get something stuck inside of you and the thought of it coming out can make you scared, but if you keep it inside, then it will hurt you and soon infection will follow. Just look at how swollen this is. Your body is trying to help you get rid of it. Remember this, whenever you keep anything bad inside of you, the same thing will happen with anger, guilt, or sadness. You have to let it out or it will destroy you. I would never do anything to hurt you. Always come to me when you have a splinter or there is something else deeper inside of here bothering you."

Pointing to my chest as she said the last part, my grandmother took my hand. I watched curiously as she pushed slightly on the sides of the splinter. It erupted in a little cloud of pus.

Looking into the expectant face of the woman, I said all the things I had kept hidden. The splinters of my life.

"Well, my boyfriend and I had a big fight. I'm not sure where we stand. I'm about to deliver my baby and I'm freaking out about how I can afford to take care of everything. I feel like my life's falling apart. I know most people feel scared about whether they will be a good mother, but I'm feeling guilty if I deserve to be a mother."

There it is, all out in the open. The woman sits back as if thinking about how to respond to my hot mess of a life.

She says, "The answer is simple. Have you prayed about this?"

I try to hide the fact that I'm disappointed. I thought she would be giving me life-changing advice instead of this.

"No. I actually haven't prayed in a very long time. It doesn't help anything."

I feel ashamed saying this though. My grandmother used to pray with me every night before bedtime. When I moved out, I promised I would still continue to pray at night. I broke that promise, in college, when I thought I was too cool for childish bedtime routines. I stopped praying because I hoped God would forget about me and not notice what I was up to.

The woman smiles as she continues, "I promise, from my own experience, it helps make things better. It sounds like you have nothing to lose. Look, why don't you stop by my church later and just give it a try. If nothing happens, at least you can say you gave it a go. That I was just some wacky woman you met at the park. What do you think?"

I don't want to offend her, so I reply, "I guess it won't hurt anything. Today is a Monday, though. There is no church today."

"You are in luck. Our church is having our last day of a special worship service. The last event is at noon today." Rolling her ankle to test it out she exclaims, "Look, my ankle is all better. I told you not to worry." Reaching into her bag she pulls out a flier for the worship service. "I really hope you take my advice. I have to get going. I'll be praying for you. Take care, okay."

I reach out and take the flier, "Alright, I'll give it a try. Nothing to lose right."

The church is easy enough to find. It is right across from the local mall, just like it said on the flier. Stalling in my car, I eat a granola bar slowly. I can't put this off any longer. Might as well say I tried and get this over with.

The music has already started when I walk in. I find a place in the back row, trying to make myself as inconspicuous as possible. Grateful the lights are dimmed, I try to make myself relax. The lyrics are on a big screen at the front. I can follow along with the band. I find myself drawn to the words as if they were written just for me.

As the singer finishes the song, my face is wet from my tears. I try to stand to leave. My legs disobey me. Shaking with the effort, I sit back down. The aching inside of me is so strong that I submit to the feeling and close my eyes. I listen to the next song and the next and so on until the show is almost over. After the band members exit the stage, the pastor of the church comes out and thanks everyone for coming. He asks, before we leave, if he can just send us out with a prayer. I close my eyes and listen to his words. Hoping that I'm worthy of God's grace and forgiveness.

Pulling into the driveway, I'm still going over the events of the day when Darcy comes storming out of her house.

"Where were you? Did you think or even care to let anybody know where you were going? Did you know how worried I was when you didn't answer my calls and I came home to find you gone?"

I've never seen Darcy this mad. I find it frightening, but I keep a level head as I reply, "I'm sorry that I didn't call you. I just needed some alone time today to think. I never meant to worry you."

Closing her eyes and taking deep breaths, she seems to calm herself before responding.

"I'm sorry, I was so worried about you. That really scared me when I didn't know what happened to you. Now that you both are back, it's all okay. I know you have been under some stress lately. It's all going to work out. You'll see. You are probably hungry. I made us some lasagna. It's my mothers recipe. I left some for you in the fridge. Why don't you eat and then get some rest. I'll be over in the morning for your check up, okay? Maybe we can get some doughnuts after you're done?"

"Thanks, Darcy. That would be nice. I'll see you in the morning."

Now she is smiling. She is back to her usual self and I'm amazed at how quickly she changed between moods.

That night, after dinner, I can hardly keep my eyes open. I fall asleep on the couch while watching TV. I barely remember getting up to use the bathroom. I crawl back into my bed with the same clothes I wore all day still on. The next morning I squint, my eyes heavy with sleep, as an energetic Darcy comes into my bedroom and pulls up the blinds. Yanking the blanket over my head from the bright light I moan inaudibly at her actions. Groaning in protest, I ask, "What are you doing?"

She still stands there hands on her hips, "Come on, you have your appointment this morning. We don't want to be late. Let's get going. I made you a breakfast smoothie. It's very nutritious, so drink up."

Slowly, I make my way into the closet to grab some clothes and get changed. I can't believe how tired I still am. This pregnancy is really catching up to me. I'm going to need a caffeine drip into my IV if I have to deliver today. Darcy insists I finish the smoothie before we leave, so to indulge her, I tip the empty cup towards her. She takes it to the sink for me. Rinsing it out, she calls over her shoulder to go to the car and she will lock up. Walking out onto the porch, I'm a little surprised at how bossy she has been today. While I wait in the car, I start to feel sleepy again and decide to recline just a little bit while I wait for Darcy. Maybe I'll close my eyes for just a second.

It feels like my eyes are taped down, as I struggle to open them. I try to reach up to feel my face but there is a pinch in my arm. Reaching over to investigate what's causing the ache, I feel something taped to my wrist.

I try to pull at it when I hear Darcy's voice, "Hey now, don't go pulling at that Elena. You need to leave it alone or I'll tie up your arm."

Slowly, my eyes open up. I can make out shapes now. I can see my body lying on a bed. I'm in a bedroom I've never seen before. Everything is quiet. As if I'm coming out of a fog, I can now focus on Darcy who is sitting on a stool at the foot of the bed. I look around the room confused. There is a wooden dresser in the corner full of picture frames of young and old people I don't know. The bedside table is at a weird position pushed almost to the wall opposite of the bed. Next to it are the cords laying on the floor to the lamp and alarm clock. A large oil painting of a doe and her fawn hangs on the wall to my left. That's when I see the IV hanging there with the tubes wrapping their way down to my arm. A needle has been inserted into my body. A clear liquid slowly drips into the tubes.

I try to speak but find my words come out squeaky, "Darcy, what's going on? Where am I?"

Darcy leans forward and pats my foot as she replies, "You are in labor silly. Now don't go messing with that IV, because if you pull it out then your contractions stop and your baby dies. We don't want that, do we?"

Disorientated, that's when I realized something about what Darcy just did that was odd. She leaned over to tap my foot. How could she have done that when she was sitting up like that on the stool? I can't even lean over to touch my own foot without bending awkwardly to the side.

That's when my eyes land on a fold up table placed in the far corner of the room, near the pine door. On the table are some towels; a box with the contents hidden from my sight; my purse; and a big beige thing. It's the big beige thing that captures my attention. I'm perplexed. My stomach realizes a second faster than my brain as it tightens up, squeezing everything into knots and sending the air right up my throat and out of me. I open my mouth wide trying to catch my breath. There, on the table, is a fake pregnant belly. It is propped up against the wall. Taped to the middle of it is the picture from the ultrasound that I gave Darcy.

Darcy

Standing in the doorway to my bedroom, I hold my hand over the lightswitch while I scan the room again, checking to make sure everything is in place. Over the weekend, I was busy making sure all the essentials for bringing a baby home were complete. In the bedroom, there is the crib and changing table. Little drawers full of diapers and wipes. A wooden shelf with tiny little clothes folded up neatly. Satisfied, I turn off the lights and check my supplies in the kitchen.

Over the weekend, I went through all the cabinets making room for formula and bottles. Next to the sink is the bottle dryer and bottle warmer. I know Tim had questioned if I planned on breastfeeding. I asked him, if he didn't mind, if we could choose formula instead. I know he was concerned with the healthiest option, but I explained I really didn't feel comfortable with the idea because of my past trauma. To appease him, I suggested I might try it after a couple days and this seemed to make him happy.

Walking into the living room, there is a bassinet set up next to the couch and a little white blanket with animals dancing hangs over the front. At the office, they gave me a gift basket for the baby. One of the nurses who does photography on the side already scheduled my baby pictures for the end of May. It seems I have everything in place.

Now, I mentally check off the preparations I've made for Elena. Nikole was able to come through for me and get the medication I needed from the hospital. Over the course of the last month. I discreetly gathered supplies from the office that I would need, like an IV hook up and sedatives. I wouldn't need pain killers. Why would I care about that?

Pulling out of the driveway, I pull my visor down as the sun shines in on me. This is going to be a perfect spring day. At lunch, I take the time to call Phillip and double check nothing has changed in his schedule. He confirms that his trip is still going as planned. He will return Wednesday afternoon.

"Perfect! I'll stop over there tomorrow and check on everything for you, okay?"

"Thank you so much, Darcy. As I said last week, this is such a short trip, I think everything will be fine until I get back."

Little does he know, he is the one helping me out this time, "Don't worry about it. It's no big deal. I find the drive out there to be very relaxing and I might just take a book if it's nice and read in the sunroom. I have an appointment in the morning so I think I'm going to just take off the whole day. You know I won't be getting much sleep soon and I want to take advantage of these last weeks."

This seems to make him happy, "Oh yes, dear, make yourself at home! You already know the guest bedroom is always there for you if you need it."

Hanging up, I think about the bag that is already packed in my trunk and ready for the trip tomorrow. This will be my second trip out there this week. Yesterday, I told Tim I wanted to run some errands and go shopping. Instead, I drove to Phillip's house and started digging in the compost pile. I severely underestimated this task. It ended up taking me six hours to dig a hole deep enough for an adult body. I could barely wrap my arms – as they throbbed from the exertion of working all day – around the bag of lime as I picked it up out of my trunk and put it in the wheelbarrow.

The hole is dug. The lime is sitting next to it. The wheelbarrow sits next to the back door ready to take the body to its final resting place. In the guest room, I have a blue plastic tarp I'll use to keep everything clean as I shove her body off the bed and drag it through the house. My fingers and back are still aching so I pop a couple painkillers into my mouth. I need to numb these sore muscles. Maybe today I'll actually walk like I'm pregnant with the way my back is strained.

Today will be my last day at work for the next three months. I'm the only one who knows this information right now. Stopping by the office before heading home, I check with the manager to make sure everything is in place and a sub is ready just in case I go into labor. The manager puts me at ease about everything and says even if I went into labor at that very moment, all would be taken care of. The time is so close. I rub my belly on the way out, waving over my shoulder, at her, as I make it home before everyone else.

I'm making a special last meal for Elena. It is my mothers lasagna recipe she went on-and-on about when we visited home, in January. I even make a small salad and breadsticks to go with it. When I check out the front window, a bit of worry starts to spread through my body. Her car still isn't back from work. Taking out my phone, I call her. There is no answer. I send her a text asking her to call me back ASAP. I know she should be out of work by this time. After about ten minutes, the lasagna is done. I take it out of the oven to cool. With no response yet, I let myself in with the spare key she gave me. I walk into her house. I try calling again and there is her phone buzzing on the table. I pick it up and see several missed calls from as early as this morning at 9am. There is a text from her office and I can only read the first couple words, *Are you coming?!* A cold sweat quickly starts forming under my armpits. I take out my phone going through the list of nearby hospitals, calling to find out if a patient was checked in maternity care that day under Elena's name. Nothing!

I try to keep myself busy and take out her piece of lasagna. Picking up the top layer of cheese, I put in the crushed sleeping pill and then put everything in her fridge and wait on the couch. The TV is off. I stare out the window for what seems like forever. Finally, after fifteen minutes, her car pulls into the driveway and she steps out alone and walks up the sidewalk.

I storm out of the house furious with her for playing these games with me. My angry outburst seems to surprise her and I have to remind myself only one more night and I won't have to deal with her anymore.

After I've collected my thoughts, I let her know about the food in the fridge. I would be there in the morning to take her to the appointment. She seems exhausted. She thanks me, as she goes back into her place. I text her that night asking about the lasagna. She thanks me saying it was delicious and that she was just going to relax on the couch and watch some TV. She would talk to me in the morning.

I could hardly sleep. I'm so excited! Today is the day. The culmination of all my planning. Throwing off the covers and bouncing out of bed, I am so happy that even Tim is caught up in my energy. I let him give me a kiss before he heads out and then I get to work making a smoothie for Elena. I put in some more crushed sleeping pills before it's all finished. I grab the letter I wrote yesterday and put it in my back pocket. The last task, before I leave today, is to take Tim's razor and tap some of the hairs around the sink. Then, I take some of his clothes and put them around the laundry hamper. In the kitchen, I take the coffee grounds and scatter them on the counter. Although it annoys me greatly to leave the house like this, I need Tim to find it like this later.

Elena doesn't answer when I knock on her door. So I let myself in. I'm surprised she is still out cold from the sleeping pills last night. She must be sensitive to that stuff. It takes some effort to get her moving. She finally gets up and gets dressed. In the kitchen I watch as she downs the whole smoothie.

"Alright, I'll wash up this cup and put away these dishes for you real quick so you can come home to a clean house. Now go get in the car. I'll be right out."

Without any arguments, she turns and I watch from the window, as I see her slowly start to nod off in the passenger seat. Her head falling over until it rests on the side window. Now I pick up pace. Going into her bedroom, I take out her suitcase and start going through drawers. I put clothes in it and in the bathroom I take her toothbrush, toothpaste and go through things quickly. I want to make it look like she left in a hurry. As I walk into the living room, pulling the suitcase behind me, I take out the letter from my back pocket and lay it down on the coffee table.

Closing the door behind me and going to the car, I put her suitcase in my trunk. I start to back out. I'm sure Elena is out cold next to me so I send a text to Tim.

> I can't believe what a mess you left the house this morning! You know how hard I've worked to make everything perfect for when the baby comes and you just don't care. Am I supposed to do it all!? I'm going to Phillip's house to calm down. I've taken the day off to relax today and don't even think about bothering me. I'll call you tomorrow to see if the house is presentable and then I'll come home. Try not to be a slob while I'm gone or you can forget about me and the baby staying there.

After I hit send, I turn my phone off. Reaching into Elena's purse, I turn her phone off too. When we pull into Phillip's wooded driveway, I guide a drowsy Elena into the guest bedroom and hook her up to the IV. It's time for me to wait. The next part is all on her.

Elena

Just when I catch my breath and go to scream, a contraction rips through my body. I grab onto the sheets. My hands are in tight fists. When the pain fades, it wakes me up enough to realize I'm in danger.

The final outcome, though not clear, to me as I plead, "Darcy, please call someone for help, I need to be in a hospital. What's going on?"

There is a change now in Darcy that I've had several quick glimpses of in the past couple months. An anger she doesn't try to hide this time. As she responds to me, small flecks of spit land on my face.

"It's time for my payback! Haven't you ever thought of the reason why you are all alone? Why you have no family and no friends? It's because people like you don't deserve happiness! Not when you rip it from the lives of others!"

I recoil from her words, "Darcy, please, I don't know what you're talking about. I'm your friend!"

She snorts at this, "Really? I thought friends don't keep secrets? Huh? I know all about your past Elena, or should I say Maria?"

This time I'm not sure what to say because even though Darcy might have found out about my past I don't know what would cause her to do this to me now. The only reason I can think of is maybe this has something to do with Liz's death. Are they related? I think back to the baby shower and I dont remember any mention about a family member who had committed suicide or someone mentoning they sure wish she could be there. Hmm… I guess they would avoid talking about her anyway and just pretend it never happened.

"Is this about Liz?"

Quickly, Darcy turns her head to me. She's standing near the table searching through items in the box.

"Who is Liz? What did you do to her, huh? Kill her baby too?"

Now I think I found the connection, "No, I didn't hurt her. Darcy, did you come to my clinic? Is this what happened to your baby? Why would you have an abortion just to take my baby. I don't understand Darcy!"

"Well, if you want to know, I actually lost my baby. I wanted that baby, but because of the botched up abortion your office gave me when I was a teenager, I can never have my own child."

As she comes around to my side I can see a little vial and clear liquid almost to the top.

"What is that Darcy?! What are you giving me?"

I try to reach out and slap her hand away from the IV bag, but I feel like I'm moving through water. My body punching against an unknown force, in slow motion. Slapping my hand down hard, she is now in my face.

"I've already given you something that will make your contractions start. If you try to stop this then you and the baby will die. Don't worry, I just want your baby. After this you are free to go."

Tears start to form in my eyes as I lower my hand. Maybe she is telling the truth. Maybe not, I don't know.

I try to plead with her again, "Darcy, this is crazy. You know I'm not responsible for what happened!"

Darcy sits back down on the stool like a guard watching her prisoner, which I guess, right now, that's exactly what I am. I start to feel the tightening in my lower abdomen again and my body tenses up. I try to count in my head to take my mind off the pain and it seems to work.

When the pain subsides I try to reason with Darcy again, "Remember all the good times we've had since we met, Darcy. We are best friends. I wont tell anyone what you did. Just please call for help. I promise I'll be there for you. You need to get help, Darcy. Please! Think of all the people in your life who love you. This will never work out. You don't want to go to jail. I'll help you."

Instead of looking worried, she seems even more at ease as she smirks at me, "Well now, that's where you misjudged me. See, I have thought this all through, every last step of the way. You see, I made sure you would have nobody to look after you. Who do you think made Noah disappear? What about everyone in the office who thinks you are a selfish brat… all accidents? No! I've already packed up your stuff in the house and left a letter explaining that you reconnected with an old flame and decided to move in with him and start fresh. See, that's what everyone already believes about you. You've already got up and left once before. It won't be too far-fetched to believe you did it again. You are right about one thing though, I do have so many people who love me. That's why they deserve this baby more than you. Who do you have for this baby? No ONE!"

I grab the sleeve of my shirt, as I wipe the tears and snot from my face, "Just tell me, are you going to kill me? You aren't going to let me go, are you?"

"I guess you are right about two things now. Don't worry, I'll take good care of your baby."

This time, I don't say anything. If she cares for this baby at all, then maybe if I can stop whatever medication is in this IV, she will be forced to get help. I pretend to be sobbing. I know this would bother her. She gets up and goes over to the box. I take this time to reach to the IV and try to yank it out. She is next to me faster than I anticipated. In her hand is a scalpel.

"Don't think I won't slit your throat right now and cut this baby out of you. The only problem is, I don't know what I'm doing and I might cut your baby too. Do you want to be the reason your baby is dead? Well?!"

Releasing the IV line, I resign to this nightmare I've woken up in. I do know one thing: I'd rather die than let anything happen to my baby. This is how my mother felt. To lose your life for the one you cared for, someone you never even met before. Darcy puts the scalpel down. She is satisfied I am now under her control.

She reaches into the box and pulls out some black rubber gloves as she tells me, "I need to see how far you are dilated."

As she is talking, another contraction starts. I don't care what she is doing at that time. The pain is controlling my every thought. Darcy slips my maternity pants off and checks me.

"Great! You are at least four centimeters dilated. This shouldn't take long after all. I was a little worried about the time. This baby has to be out by tomorrow afternoon. That's when Phillip will be back. He will be pleasantly surprised to find me here with my little baby. You see there is no service here. Poor me will have gone into labor and couldn't leave to get to a good service spot. So I'll have to deliver my own baby by myself. Just think of how brave everyone will think I was!"

As I'm laying down, I turn my head. I'm staring at the painting. Anything to get my mind off the present situation I'm in. I imagine I'm there in the forest with the doe. I'm showing the fawn to my own child. Noah is there too. We are one happy family. That's when I feel the blanket under me start to get damp as warm liquid starts to pool around my lower abdomen. It's like I've peed myself.

My water just broke. I know it won't be long now. The contractions start getting stronger and closer together. As I lay there, the contractions come and go. I focus on the painting, imagining I'm somewhere else. I don't know what time it is, but I try to keep track of the sunlight coming in from the window. The shadow it casts off the furniture moving slowly across the floor. It has to be close to 3pm by now.

When Darcy checks me again, she tells me I'm now eight centimeters dilated. I can tell she is starting to get excited. At this point, I don't care anymore. I close my eyes and choose to focus on happy moments from my life. If im about to die, then I might as well not worry about the stupid things now. I focus on memories of my grandmother. Her warm hugs; Her voice as she read me stories; how she always got me to eat new foods by putting maple syrup on it. I think about Noah and how we held on to each other after making love. How it seemed we were the only people in the world. I wish I could have one more minute with him so I could tell him I love him.

The next contraction starts and my stomach tenses.

As the muscles pull together, I reach out to Darcy, "Please, just get it over with. Kill me now. I'm ready to go."

Instead, she sits up and stretches out her arms over her head and rolls her neck.

"I guess it's almost showtime."

Getting off the stool, she lays out the towels and starts setting out items next to it. I mostly keep my eyes shut. When I try to make out what she has planned for me, I can see scissors, a bulb looking instrument, and a little bottle of sleeping pills.

With the next contraction, the pressure starts to build. I think I need to use the restroom. Darcy has me lay back. She makes me spread my legs and she looks up at me excitedly.

"I can see the head!"

There is no thought of before or after. All I can think about is right now as contractions pummel me. My muscles tighten and pull. I can feel my body open up. The pressure starts to intensify. Darcy tells me to start pushing with each contraction. With only a cotton blanket to comfort me, I grab it with both hands and press down. I push for what feels like forever. I feel like my body is being stretched wide open. The baby's head crowns and I scream out, in pain, as the burning sensation tears through my body.

With another contraction, I push again and Darcy yells at me, "The head is out, come on another push!"

With what seems to be the last of my strength, I grit my teeth. A bead of sweat drips into my eye and I force this little person out into the world. I try to stay on my elbows so I can look at my baby, but my body gives way and I fall back. I'm exhausted and shaky. Now taking the scissors, Darcy cuts through the umbilical cord and whisks my baby away.

She starts rubbing towels over the little body. All I can see is the tiny head. There are thick black curls covering it. Darcy's body blocks my view from the rest. She takes the bulb-like instrument and starts sucking to clean the little nose. I assume it must have been an aspirator. I vaguely remember getting one in an infant care kit. At this the head moves around and I see a little hand come up. The baby seems to suck in a deep breath and then lets out the most glorious cry. If a child's laughter was medicine for the soul, an infant's cry is medicine for my broken body. The pain seems to dissolve and my heart bursts with love and concern. Even though it's only been seconds, my body yearns to be close to my child again. I know I have to let these dreams go. That is the deal I made with the devil. My child will live. I will die.

With her back to me, Darcy wraps my baby in a tight swaddle. She takes the little bundle and places it down on the floor next to the dresser. Darcy now turns to me. She walks back to the table and grabs the sleeping pills and a water bottle. Placing four of the little white pills in my hand she passes me the water bottle.

"Here swallow these and it will all be over soon. When you are sleeping, I'll suffocate you and you won't even feel a thing. I'll bury you outside in the compost pile and your body will be used to make fertilizer. Quite the appropriate way to give back to the plants you love so much. By the way, I'll take good care of your baby and I just want to thank you for taking care of both of my babies for me these past couple months."

I give her a confused face and she leans closer and whispers into my ear, "I buried my baby in your peace lilies planter. I'll be back to get that baby too, when you're gone."

At this point I know there is no reasoning with Darcy, she has completely lost her mind. Taking the pills, my hand shakes so much they fall onto the bed. She has to pick them back up off the blanket and place them in my mouth for me. My mouth is so dry. They stick to my tongue and I swallow almost half the contents of the bottle trying to get them down.

It doesn't seem like a long time waiting for the effects of the pills to start. My body is already completely drained… both physically and mentally. A slight contraction pushes the rest of my placenta out. As I try to sit up and look at my baby for one last time, a little arm has wrangled out of the blanket and a hand shoots straight up. I reach out wishing I could just touch those little fingers and say goodbye. Darcy has her back to me. She is pulling a tarp out of the box and putting other things away. Closing my eyes I send out a prayer, nothing to lose right.

"God, I know I don't deserve your help. Please forgive me. If you are out there, please look over my baby."

I notice the sunlight has now cast long shadows in the room and the sun is almost setting. A sliver of sunlight now rests on my lower body. It glistens off something on the bed. I look a little closer and realize I may be able to save myself.

Noah

My fingers hover over her name on my phone. I end up turning it off and put it away. I have a rare break, in my schedule, today. I'm left with my thoughts to torment me. The sun is starting to rise, but I don't feel like getting out of bed. Even though I'm so hurt by what Darcy told me, I can't seem to shake this feeling that something is not right. The thing I don't understand, though, is why Darcy would say that. There has to be some truth because Elena has been keeping something from me. I need to know the truth. My pride gets in the way every time I try to call her.

Now, there is a buzzing from my hoodie pocket. I hurriedly reach in and pull my phone out. It's my mom.

Deflated, I answer her, "Hey."

I told her everything last week. She is the only person in my family who knows. She has been texting me everyday for an update.

"Hey, any news yet?"

I know my mother is holding back on giving me advice and this is hard on her too. Not knowing if she is going to be a grandmother or not. She doesn't like to see me hurting.

"Nothing yet. I just don't understand. I really thought I knew what kind of person she was. I'm so confused. The thing that keeps getting me is why would Darcy say this if it wasn't true. Elena is holding something back. I don't think it's what Darcy is saying. There is something else she has done, but it's not someone else. What we had was just so..."

There are no words for what we had, my mother replies, "Some people just like to make trouble. There is no way to understand them. If you did, then you would be like them. And that's not you. I know you. I can tell Elena is a good person, too. Maybe the best thing is to go to her and talk about everything. Work this out. If this baby does turn out to be yours, I know you will regret not being there for the birth. Sometimes you can't take things back. If there is some misunderstanding and you and Elena do get back together, deserting her will always be a source of resentment in your relationship. Go to her."

My mother has never led me wrong before. In this case she is probably right. so I agree.

"Alright, I'll text you later with an update."

Hanging up, I close my eyes and push down on Elenas number. It goes straight to voicemail. I send a text and wait but no response. I try to call Darcy and it goes straight to voicemail too.

Well, no more waiting around. I pull up a travel app and find out I can get a flight leaving at 12:00 pm. After layovers, I could be there by 4:00 pm. While I get ready, I try again. No answer. This time I search for the name of the clinic where Elena works. I get a hold of a lady named Jackie.

"Hey, I'm looking for Elena. This is her boyfriend, Noah."

There is a slight pause before the lady speaks again, "We would like to know the same thing. She hasn't been to work today or yesterday. If you do get in touch with her, let her know we have a replacement and her help isn't needed here anyway."

At this, she hangs up. I feel bad for Elena working with someone so callous. Isn't she even worried about her pregnant co-worker being missing for two days? Now, I call the nursing agency to see if they can get me in touch with Darcy and the manager, Missy, picks up.

I ask her, " Hey! This is Noah. I was wondering if Darcy is in today? I have been trying to get in touch with her."

She excitedly replies, "Hey, Noah! Hope everything is going well for you! Actually, Darcy didn't come in today. She texted me that she was very tired and wanted to relax. Isn't it so exciting? I bet she is going to be having her baby very soon!"

Furrowing my brow, in worry, I reply, "Yeah, sure, Bye."

I can't sit around and wait. Something is wrong. I have to get to Elena now. I get into my car and start my way back to Cincinnati.

Managing to make it with only one stop for gas, I pull into the duplex driveway around 3:00 pm. Elena's car is still in the driveway. Darcy and Tim are gone. I know Elena hid a spare key on the underside of her wicker chair. When I reach under, my fingers find the tape and I rip the key down.

Once inside her house, I call out to her. There is no response. In the bedroom, the dresser drawer is pulled open and clothes are strewn about the floor. Walking back out, my heart breaks when I see a pyramid of boxes full of baby items unopened. A little baby romper hanging from the top, like a star on the top of a christmas tree, has the words Im proof my mommy loves nurses. As I'm getting ready to head out the front door, my sight catches on a letter on the coffee table. It is addressed to Darcy. I grab it looking for clues.

Darcy,

I know this is pretty crappy of me to do. I'm leaving. Being here and raising this baby without Noah is too much for me. I reconnected with someone from Texas who will take care of us. Sorry to let you down. You have been such a great friend and helped me with everything. This is just what I do. When things get rough it's best to start over somewhere else. So I'm looking for a fresh start and I hope the best for you. Enjoy your new little one, you deserve it!

XOXO ELENA

Reading the letter again, it just doesn't seem right to me. Although it sounds like Elena, I don't know why she wouldn't take any of her possessions from the house. Why would she leave her car? Panic starts seeping into my stomach. I can't shake it. I need to find Elena now. Walking out, a dejected looking Tim comes up the steps of his place at the same time. Glancing over at me he nods and his usual cheery self is gone.

"Hey, Noah. Didn't expect to see you around. Darcy said you and Elena broke up or something."

"I'm back. I need to find Elena. She isn't at work. Can you try calling Darcy? They might be together."

Tim looks down at his shoes as he replies, "I made Darcy pretty mad today. I guess I left the place a mess and she told me not to call her because she needed space from me. I took off this afternoon to clean the house so she will come home. I don't know where Elena is."

Taking my hand, I point to the car in the driveway. Tim looks in the direction as if just realizing.

"Her car is still here Tim! She must have gone with Darcy. Where did she go?"

Now Tim is thinking about the possibility, "I guess she could be with her, but I can't get a hold of them. They wouldn't have service where they are. Somewhere outside of town at Darcy's patient's house in the country. Phillip is all I know. She rarely talks about patient stuff. The confidentiality rules you know."

"We are going there right now. Let's go."

I walk briskly to the car and Tim seems to be unsure of what to do. He turns and follows me, getting into the passenger seat.

It's almost closing time, 4:45 pm, as we pull into the office parking lot. Missy looks surprised to see me after just talking on the phone that morning.

"Noah, hey, what are you doing?"

Walking up to the counter, there is no time for niceties as I ask, "Missy, I need to know the address for one of Darcy's patients.

He lives in the country. A guy named Phillip. It would be pretty far out of town. A place without cell service. I'm betting it is a patient not many people would want to take because of the drive. Darcy might be in labor and her friend might be in danger too. We need to get there now."

At this, Missy looks between Tim and me alarmed, "Oh my! Let me get it for you!"

Getting on her laptop, she quickly writes the address down on a sticky note and hands it to me.

"Do you want me to send an ambulance too, just in case?"

Grabbing the sticky note and heading for the door I call out to her, "Yes! I'll meet them there!"

Driving as fast as the back country roads allow, my GPS says there is twenty minutes left of the drive. As we get to the top of a hill, my phone loses service off and on as the trees whiz past my window. Tim and I drive in silence. My fear is spreading to him. Soon he is chewing on his nails and asking if we can go any faster.

Elena

Slowing my breathing, I close my eyes and pretend to have already fallen asleep. Darcy comes around and removes the needle from my arm. I can hear her taking down the IV stand. Listening to her retreating steps, I open my eyes and slowly start to sit up. Ignoring the pain, I reach down and grab the umbilical cord. I'm too scared to be grossed out. It feels like soggy, raw sausage forming one long link. It's slimy, so I use some of the cotton sheet to wipe it dry. My eyes are fixed on Darcy. I wipe off the cord where I'll need to grab it. Hopefully it gives me the traction to hold on.

Summoning every last ounce of strength and all my will to protect my child, a lightning bolt of adrenaline kicks in. I get my legs under me as if I'm a bullfrog. I can hardly believe it. Darcy starts to hum. So confident in her planning. She isn't paying attention to me at all. She has let her guard down.

I leap from the bed and land squarely on her back, wrapping the cord around her neck. I pull it as tight as I can. She falls back. She is trying to push me off. She swings her arms around trying to hit me. My back hits the floor hard, but the pain only serves as a boost to my system. It seems to revive me. As I'm on the floor, I wrap my legs around her. I bring her as close to my body as I can. I cry out as pain tears through my body. I can feel blood gushing out of me. I turn my head and focus on the little arm swinging in the air cheering me on. I pull as tight as I can on the umbilical cord. Blackness begins creeping into my periphery. My body threatens to shut down if I don't stop. Like a computer overheating, my body has reached limits. Either I'll stop or my body will force me to. There is no way I can let go though. Even if this kills me.

I know my baby will survive until Phillip comes back tomorrow afternoon. I remember being amazed when I read infants can sometimes go one to two days without fluids. I'm sure my little one will survive. Then, everyone will know the truth. Noah will raise our baby. Those happy holiday memories I had envisioned for the future will be intact. Even if I'm not in them.

I hold on until my arms start to ache and the room begins to spin. I can feel Darcy go limp in my arms. I fight to stay awake, holding on with everything I have. Counting in my head, from one to ten, I repeat over and over. I try to remain focused. I can feel my body start to give way. The umbilical cord comes apart. My arms come flying back and slap the floor. Darcy's full weight is on me. I dont have the strength to push her off. My head lags to the side just as I'm about to pass out.

I realize I must be already dreaming because Noah's face is in front of mine. He is saying my name and I reach out to touch him amazed.

My voice barely audible, "I love you."

Blackness invades me.

POSTPARTUM CARE

Elena

Peeking out of the side room of the church, I can see the pews are filled with people. Noah is nowhere in sight. Probably still in the back waiting until the pastor announces it's time to get started. Smoothing down the front of my beaded gown, I don't even care if there is still a little belly there. With all I went through, I'm just grateful to be alive.

It's crazy to believe three months have already passed since that day. It feels like yesterday. I know people always say that, but it's true. I sleep with the lights on in the house. I double-check everything is locked.

Things are all patched up with everyone at the outpatient clinic. I no longer work there. I'm there now as a patient. I see Lynn, the same woman who used to buy me muffins. She is helping me see my way through my experience. We both have confidence that one day I'll be able to look back and not hold any fear.

I almost died that day. There are only two reasons I survived: God and Noah. The ambulance came shortly after Noah arrived and rushed me to the hospital. I had lost a lot of blood and was unconscious for almost two days. I remember waking up at one point during that time. I urged my eyes to stay open. I could see Noah rocking a little pink bundle in the corner. That image lulled me back to sleep peacefully. I could start to relax and heal.

When I finally came to, I sat up slowly in bed. It had felt like someone put me in one of those old torture devices where they stretched out the prisoners limbs. Every part of my body screamed in protest as I moved. I still fought through it to hold my baby girl. I brought her close to my face and breathed in her smell. I kissed her little head as that little arm came up again. This time in celebration. We had won!

Noah was at my side the entire time. When he wasn't apologizing with words, his eyes would look at me and remorse was all over his face. Our first night home from the hospital, I took down the box and spilled all my secrets to him. I let it all out in his arms. As I cried, I divulged fears, anger, guilt, sadness and regret. He just held me and stroked my hair. There are no more secrets between us now. Just unconditional love.

Knowing Darcy passed away is something I'll have to live with for the rest of my life. Noah reminds me there is no reason to blame myself for what happened. It was in self-defense. I still wish there was another way. The person I feel the worst for, though, is Tim. He lost his wife that day and his hopes for a child. An entire family… an entire future torn away from him.

We have already spoken. He came to the hospital to let me know he was moving back to his hometown. He did not blame me for what happened. Maybe we both are living with guilt for not seeing the signs and being able to help Darcy. I told him about the peace lilies planter and he said it would be too hard on him to see it everyday. I promised him I would take care of it and make sure a flower always flourished in that planter in memory of his child.

As I glance out into the room, I can see Noah now standing at the front of the church. We were here last month to give our lives to God. Today we give our lives to each other.

The doctors in the hospital didn't want to comment too much on what I went through. They mentioned it was very uncommon for umbilical cords to be as long as mine and to have the tensile strength that mine did. In other words, I know they were shocked by the fact that I choked someone with an umbilical cord. I knew God had a plan all along. The key to my survival was growing in me. The very thing that gave my daughter life also gave me life. Ironically, it took someone else's.

I won't dwell on the past. I only have my future to look forward to. My daughter, dressed in a pink lace gown with a white headband, sleeps peacefully in the arms of Noah's mother in the front pew.

I shut the door and slowly walk over to the small loveseat in the dressing room. There is one last person not in attendance. I pick up my bouquet and the frame of my grandmother holding me as a child. Today she is walking me down the aisle.

As I stare down lovingly at the picture, I notice it must have moved on the ride over. The picture is slightly off-kilter. In the top corner another picture seems to be placed directly behind this one. Curious, I flip the frame over and take off the back. Moving it aside I can see the picture has an inscription in my grandmother's handwriting on the back.

Bless this child, Dear God, and Bless her children, and her children's children, all the days of their lives. May you always watch over them, Amen.

— Angelina and her precious baby girl

I run my fingers over the words and smile. Gently, I pick up the picture and turn it over. The color has faded over the years, but it's the same rocking chair and background as the image from my grandmother and I. As I look at the little girl, who must be my mother, I find myself hoping to see some resemblance in my own daughter someday. When I look at the whole picture, my breath catches. I move my hand to my mouth in shock. I knew I had seen the young woman from the park before. My grandmother, when she was in her early 20's, and the woman from the park are the same person. I was never truly alone. My grandmother was there to help me just as she promised. My own guardian angel.

Lifting my head up, I know without a doubt, I will never be alone. I will not be afraid anymore. All my sins and fears have been forgiven and washed away. I am a new person. I deserve to live in peace and prosper.

"Thank you, God. Thank you, grandmother."

As I put the frame back together, I stand. The door opens in front of me. Noah's father motions for me. It's time to begin. I walk out into the light. The sun shines down from the stained glass window and rainbows of color dance across my vision and my future.

THE END

My intentions, with this story, are not based on pro-life or pro-choice. I'm not here to pass any kind of judgment. It's simply a story I was motivated to write. I wanted to let people know some consequences abortion can have on women.

While doing some research for this story, I was surprised to find proven studies that show the increased risk of suicide, depression, substance abuse, anxiety and mental health issues after a woman has gone through with an abortion.

It seems the focus is always on the babies, which is heartbreaking, too. Nobody talks about how harmful it can be to a woman. We have the amazing ability to bring life into this world. It is truly a life changing gift from God. I would never encourage someone I love to throw that special gift away because of the damage it could do to their mental health and their life. Instead, I hope to be a pillar of support and be there for them.

I hope this book lets you know you have a heavenly father who loves you and supports you with an unlimited supply of forgiveness. I know, personally, the love and blessings God provides, through Jesus. I have seen, with my own eyes, how he can change people and circumstances most would have given up hope on. Please know you are not alone and there are people who care and love you.

For more information on how God can work in your life please check out the website: **lifehopeandtruth.com**

-Danielle

Dedication/Acknowledgements

This book is dedicated to women.

My mother, mother-in-law, step-mother, grandmother, aunts, cousins, friends, sisters, nieces and daughter. You have shaped me into the person I am today. When I wrote this book, I thought of you all. I want you to know there isn't a day that goes by that you are not on my mind. I love you all so much. Thank you for everything!

Thanks to Brett for his amazing proofreading skills and taking his time to make my writing shine. Thank you to everyone who listened to me as I talked endlessly about my story and for all the support. Thanks to my husband for believing in me and for taking on the meals and childcare so I could have quiet time to myself.

Thank you to God for giving me this talent and passion for reading and storytelling.